LIKE WATER FOR CHOCOLATE

Translated by

Carol Christensen

and

Thomas Christensen

D O U B L E D A Y

New York ❖ *London* ❖ *Toronto*

Sydney ❖ *Auckland*

LIKE

WATER

FOR

CHOCOLATE

A Novel in Monthly

Installments,

with Recipes, Romances,

and Home Remedies

LAURA ESQUIVEL

Published by Doubleday, a division of
Bantam Doubleday Dell Publishing Group, Inc.

DOUBLEDAY and the portrayal of an anchor with
a dolphin are trademarks of Doubleday,
a division of Bantam Doubleday Dell
Publishing Group, Inc.

Book design by Marysarah Quinn

Cover painting © 1992 Cathleen Toelke

Cover design by Julie Duquet

Library of Congress information available upon request.

This translation is for Claire and Ellen.

ISBN 978-0-307-29199-8

Printed in the United States of America

10 9 8 7 6 5 4 3 2 1

LIKE WATER FOR CHOCOLATE

To the table or to bed
You must come when you are bid.

CHAPTER ONE

JANUARY

Christmas Rolls

INGREDIENTS:

1 can of sardines
1/2 chorizo sausage
1 onion
oregano
1 can of chiles serranos
10 hard rolls

PREPARATION:

Take care to chop the onion fine. To keep from crying when you chop it (which is so annoying!), I suggest you place a little bit on your head. The trouble with crying over an onion is that once the chopping gets you started and the tears begin to well up, the next thing you know you just can't stop. I don't know whether that's ever happened to you, but I have to confess it's happened to me, many times. Mama used to say it was because I was especially sensitive to onions, like my great-aunt, Tita.

Tita was so sensitive to onions, any time they were being chopped, they say she would just cry and cry; when she was still in my great-grandmother's belly her sobs were so loud that even Nacha, the cook, who was half-deaf, could hear them easily. Once her wailing got so violent that it brought on an early labor. And before my great-grandmother could let out a word or even a whimper, Tita made her entrance into this world, prematurely, right there on the kitchen table amid the smells of simmering noodle soup, thyme, bay leaves, and cilantro, steamed milk, garlic, and, of course, onion. Tita had no need for the usual slap on the bottom, because she was already crying as she emerged; maybe that was because she knew then that it would be her lot in life to be denied marriage. The way Nacha told it, Tita was literally washed into this world on a great tide of tears that spilled over the edge of the table and flooded across the kitchen floor.

That afternoon, when the uproar had subsided and the water had been dried up by the sun, Nacha swept up the residue the tears had left on the red stone floor. There was enough salt to fill a ten-pound sack—it was used for cooking and lasted a long time. Thanks to her unusual birth, Tita felt a deep love for the kitchen, where she spent most of her life from the day she was born.

When she was only two days old, Tita's father, my great-grandfather, died of a heart attack and Mama Elena's milk dried up from the shock. Since there was no such thing as powdered milk in those days, and they couldn't find a wet nurse anywhere, they were in a panic to satisfy the infant's hunger. Nacha, who knew everything about cooking—and much more that doesn't enter the picture until later—offered to take charge of feeding Tita. She felt she had the best chance of "educating the innocent child's stomach," even though she had never married or had children. Though she didn't know how to read or write, when it came to cooking she knew everything there was to know. Mama Elena accepted her offer gratefully; she had enough to do between her mourning and the enormous responsibility of running the ranch—

and it was the ranch that would provide her children the food and education they deserved—without having to worry about feeding a newborn baby on top of everything else.

From that day on, Tita's domain was the kitchen, where she grew vigorous and healthy on a diet of teas and thin corn gruels. This explains the sixth sense Tita developed about everything concerning food. Her eating habits, for example, were attuned to the kitchen routine: in the morning, when she could smell that the beans were ready; at midday, when she sensed the water was ready for plucking the chickens; and in the afternoon, when the dinner bread was baking, Tita knew it was time for her to be fed.

Sometimes she would cry for no reason at all, like when Nacha chopped onions, but since they both knew the cause of those tears, they didn't pay them much mind. They made them a source of entertainment, so that during her childhood Tita didn't distinguish between tears of laughter and tears of sorrow. For her laughing was a form of crying.

Likewise for Tita the joy of living was wrapped up in the delights of food. It wasn't easy for a person whose knowledge of life was based on the kitchen to comprehend the outside world. That world was an endless expanse that began at the door between the kitchen and the rest of the house, whereas everything on the kitchen side of that door, on through the door leading to the patio and the kitchen and herb gardens was completely hers—it was Tita's realm.

Her sisters were just the opposite: to them, Tita's world seemed full of unknown dangers, and they were terrified of it. They felt that playing in the kitchen was foolish and dangerous. But once, Tita managed to convince them to join her in watching the dazzling display made by dancing water drops dribbled on a red hot griddle.

While Tita was singing and waving her wet hands in time, showering drops of water down on the griddle so they would "dance," Rosaura was cowering in the corner, stunned by the display. Gertrudis, on the other hand, found this game enticing, and she threw herself into it with the enthusiasm she always showed where rhythm, movement, or music were involved. Then Rosaura had tried to join them—but since she barely moistened her hands and then shook them gingerly, her efforts didn't have the desired effect. So Tita tried to move her hands closer to the griddle. Rosaura resisted, and they struggled for control until Tita became annoyed and let go, so that momentum carried Rosaura's hands onto it. Tita got a terrible spanking for that, and she was forbidden to play with her sisters in her own, world. Nacha became her playmate then. Together they made up all sorts of games and activities having to do with cooking. Like the day they saw a man in the village plaza twisting long thin balloons into animal shapes, and they decided to do it with sausages. They didn't just make real animals, they also made up some of their own, creatures with the neck of a swan, the legs of a dog, the tail of a horse, and on and on.

Then there was trouble, however, when the animals had to be taken apart to fry the sausage. Tita refused to do it. The only time she was willing to take them apart was when the sausage was intended for the Christmas rolls she loved so much. Then she not only allowed her animals to be dismantled, she watched them fry with glee.

The sausage for the rolls must be fried over very low heat, so that it cooks thoroughly without getting too brown. When done, remove from the heat and add the sardines, which have been deboned ahead of time. Any black spots on the skin should also have been scraped off with a knife. Combine the onions, chopped chiles, and the ground oregano with the sardines. Let the mixture stand before filling the rolls.

Tita enjoyed this step enormously; while the filling was resting, it was very pleasant to savor its aroma, for smells have the power to evoke the past, bringing back sounds and even other smells that have no match in the present. Tita liked to take a deep breath and let the characteristic smoke and smell transport her through the recesses of her memory.

It was useless to try to recall the first time she had smelled one of those rolls—she couldn't, possibly because it had been before she was born. It might have been the unusual combination of sardines and sausages that had called to her and made her decide to trade the peace of ethereal existence in Mama Elena's belly for life as her daughter, in order to enter the De la Garza family and share their delicious meals and wonderful sausage.

On Mama Elena's ranch, sausage making was a real ritual. The day before, they started peeling garlic, cleaning chiles, and grinding spices. All the women in the family had to participate: Mama Elena; her daughters, Gertrudis, Rosaura, and Tita; Nacha, the cook; and Chencha, the maid. They gathered around the dining-room table in the afternoon, and between the talking and the joking the time flew by until it started to get dark. Then Mama Elena would say:

"That's it for today."

For a good listener, it is said, a single word will suffice, so when they heard that, they all sprang into action. First they had to clear the table; then they had to assign tasks: one collected the chickens, another drew water for breakfast from the well, a third was in charge of wood for the stove. There would be no ironing, no embroidery, no sewing that day. When it was all finished, they went to their bedrooms to read, say their prayers, and go to sleep. One afternoon, before Mama Elena told them they could leave the table, Tita, who was then fifteen, announced in a trembling voice that Pedro Muzquiz would like to come and speak with her. . . .

After an endless silence during which Tita's soul shrank, Mama Elena asked:

"And why should this gentleman want to come talk to me?"

Tita's answer could barely be heard:

"I don't know."

Mama Elena threw her a look that seemed to Tita to contain all the years of repression that had flowed over the family, and said:

"If he intends to ask for your hand, tell him not to bother. He'll be wasting his time and mine too. You know perfectly well that being the youngest daughter means you have to take care of me until the day I die."

With that Mama Elena got slowly to her feet, put her glasses in her apron, and said in a tone of final command:

"That's it for today."

Tita knew that discussion was not one of the forms of communication permitted in Mama Elena's household, but even so, for the first time in her life, she intended to protest her mother's ruling.

"But in my opinion . . ."

"You don't have an opinion, and that's all I want to hear about it. For generations, not a single person in my family has ever questioned this tradition, and no daughter of mine is going to be the one to start."

Tita lowered her head, and the realization of her fate struck her as forcibly as her tears struck the table. From then on they knew, she and the table, that they could never have even the slightest voice in the unknown forces that fated Tita to bow before her mother's absurd decision, and the table to continue to receive the bitter tears that she had first shed on the day of her birth.

Still Tita did not submit. Doubts and anxieties sprang to her mind. For one thing, she wanted to know who started this family tradition. It would be nice if she could let that genius know about one little flaw in this perfect plan for taking care of women in their old age. If Tita couldn't marry and have children, who would take care of her when she got old? Was there a solution in a case like that? Or are daughters who stay home and take care of their mothers not expected to survive too long after the parent's death? And what about women who marry and can't have children, who will take care of them? And besides, she'd like to know what kind of studies had established that the youngest daughter and not the eldest is best suited to care for their mother. Had the opinion of the daughter affected by the plan ever been taken into account? If she couldn't marry, was she at least allowed to experience love? Or not even that?

Tita knew perfectly well that all these questions would have to be buried forever in the archive of questions that have no answers. In the De la Garza family, one obeyed—immediately. Ignoring Tita completely, a very angry Mama Elena left the kitchen, and for the next week she didn't speak a single word to her.

What passed for communication between them resumed when Mama Elena, who was inspecting the clothes each of the women had been sewing, discovered that Tita's creation, which was the most perfect, had not been basted before it was sewed.

"Congratulations," she said, "your stitches are perfect —but you didn't baste it, did you?"

"No," answered Tita, astonished that the sentence of silence had been revoked.

"Then go and rip it out. Baste it and sew it again and then come and show it to me. And remember that the lazy man and the stingy man end up walking their road twice."

"But that's if a person makes a mistake, and you yourself said a moment ago that my sewing was . . ."

"Are you starting up with your rebelliousness again? It's enough that you have the audacity to break the rules in your sewing."

"I'm sorry, Mami. I won't ever do it again."

With that Tita succeeded in calming Mama Elena's anger. For once she had been very careful; she had called her "Mami" in the correct tone of voice. Mama Elena felt that the word *Mama* had a disrespectful sound to it, and so, from the time they were little, she had ordered her daughters to use the word *Mami* when speaking to her. The only one who resisted, the only one who said the word without the proper deference was Tita, which had earned her plenty of slaps. But how perfectly she had said it this time! Mama Elena took comfort in the hope that she had finally managed to subdue her youngest daughter.

Unfortunately her hope was short-lived, for the very next day Pedro Muzquiz appeared at the house, his esteemed father at his side, to ask for Tita's hand in marriage. His arrival caused a huge uproar, as his visit was completely unexpected. Several days earlier Tita had sent Pedro a message via Nacha's brother asking him to abandon his suit. The brother swore he had delivered the message to Pedro, and yet, there they were, in the house. Mama Elena received them in the living room; she was extremely polite and explained why it was impossible for Tita to marry.

"But if you really want Pedro to get married, allow me to suggest my daughter Rosaura, who's just two years older than Tita. *She* is one hundred percent available, and ready for marriage. . . ."

At that Chencha almost dropped right onto Mama Elena the tray containing coffee and cookies, which she had carried into the living room to offer don Pascual and his son. Excusing herself, she rushed back to the kitchen, where Tita, Rosaura, and Gertrudis were waiting for her to fill them in on every detail about what was going on in the living room. She burst headlong into the room, and they all immediately stopped what they were doing, so as not to miss a word she said.

They were together in the kitchen making Christmas Rolls. As the name implies, these rolls are usually prepared around Christmas, but today they were being prepared in honor of Tita's birthday. She would soon be sixteen years old, and she wanted to celebrate with one of her favorite dishes.

"Isn't that something? Your ma talks about being ready for marriage like she was dishing up a plate of enchiladas! And the worse thing is, they're completely different! You can't just switch tacos and enchiladas like that!"

Chencha kept up this kind of running commentary as she told the others—in her own way, of course—about the scene she had just witnessed. Tita knew Chencha sometimes exaggerated and distorted things, so she held her aching heart in check. She would not accept what she had just heard. Feigning calm, she continued cutting the rolls for her sisters and Nacha to fill.

It is best to use homemade rolls. Hard rolls can easily be obtained from a bakery, but they should be small; the larger ones are unsuited for this recipe. After filling the rolls, bake for ten minutes and serve hot. For best results, leave the rolls out overnight, wrapped in a cloth, so that the grease from the sausage soaks into the bread.

When Tita was finishing wrapping the next day's rolls, Mama Elena came into the kitchen and informed them that she had agreed to Pedro's marriage—to Rosaura.

Hearing Chencha's story confirmed, Tita felt her body fill with a wintry chill: in one sharp, quick blast she was so cold and dry her cheeks burned and turned red, red as the apples beside her. That overpowering chill lasted a long time, and she could find no respite, not even when Nacha told her what she had overheard as she escorted don Pascual Muzquiz and his son to the ranch's gate. Nacha followed them, walking as quietly as she could in order to hear the conversation between father and son. Don Pascual and Pedro were walking slowly, speaking in low, controlled, angry voices.

"Why did you do that, Pedro? It will look ridiculous, your agreeing to marry Rosaura. What happened to the eternal love you swore to Tita? Aren't you going to keep that vow?"

"Of course I'll keep it. When you're told there's no way you can marry the woman you love and your only hope of being near her is to marry her sister, wouldn't you do the same?"

Nacha didn't manage to hear the answer; Pulque, the ranch dog, went running by, barking at a rabbit he mistook for a cat.

"So you intend to marry without love?"

"No, Papa, I am going to marry with a great love for Tita that will never die."

Their voices grew less and less audible, drowned out by the crackling of dried leaves beneath their feet. How strange that Nacha, who was quite hard of hearing by that time, should have claimed to have heard this conversation. Still, Tita thanked Nacha for telling her—but that did not alter the icy feelings she began to have for Pedro. It is said that the deaf can't hear but can understand. Perhaps Nacha only heard what everyone else was afraid to say. Tita could not get to sleep that night; she could not find the words for what she was feeling. How unfortunate that black holes in space had not yet been discovered, for then she might have understood the black hole in the center of her chest, infinite coldness flowing through it.

Whenever she closed her eyes she saw scenes from last Christmas, the first time Pedro and his family had been invited to dinner; the scenes grew more and more vivid, and the cold within her grew sharper. Despite the time that had passed since that evening, she remembered it perfectly: the sounds, the smells, the way her new dress had grazed the freshly waxed floor, the look Pedro gave her . . . That look! She had been walking to the table carrying a tray of egg-yolk candies when she first felt his hot gaze burning her skin. She turned her head, and her eyes met Pedro's. It was then she understood how dough feels when it is plunged into boiling oil. The heat that invaded her body was so real she was afraid she would start to bubble—her face, her stomach, her heart, her breasts—like batter, and unable to endure his gaze she lowered her eyes and hastily crossed the room, to where Gertrudis was pedaling the player piano, playing a waltz called "The Eyes of Youth." She set her tray on a little table in the middle of the room, picked up a glass of Noyo liquor that was in front of her, hardly aware of what she was doing, and sat down next to Paquita Lobo, the De la Garzas' neighbor. But even that distance between herself and Pedro was not enough; she felt her blood pulsing, searing her veins. A deep flush suffused her face and no matter how she tried she could not find a place for her eyes to rest. Paquita saw that something was bothering her, and with a look of great concern, she asked:

"That liquor is pretty strong, isn't it?"

"Pardon me?"

"You look a little woozy, Tita. Are you feeling all right?"

"Yes, thank you."

"You're old enough to have a little drink on a special occasion, but tell me, you little devil, did your mama say it was okay? I can see you're excited—you're shaking— and I'm sorry but I must say you'd better not have any more. You wouldn't want to make a fool of yourself."

That was the last straw! To have Paquita Lobo think she was drunk. She couldn't allow the tiniest suspicion to remain in Paquita's mind or she might tell her mother. Tita's fear of her mother was enough to make her forget Pedro for a moment, and she applied herself to convincing Paquita, any way she could, that she was thinking clearly, that her mind was alert. She chatted with her, she gossiped, she made small talk. She even told her the recipe for this Noyo liquor which was supposed to have had such an effect on her. The liquor is made by soaking four ounces of peaches and a half pound of apricots in water for twenty-four hours to loosen the skin; next, they are peeled, crushed, and steeped in hot water for fifteen days. Then the liquor is distilled. After two and a half pounds of sugar have been completely dissolved in the water, four ounces of orange-flower water are added, and the mixture is stirred and strained. And so there would be no lingering doubts about her mental and physical well-being, she reminded Paquita, as if it were just an aside, that the water containers held 2.016 liters, no more and no less.

So when Mama Elena came over to ask Paquita if she was being properly entertained, she replied enthusiastically.

"Oh yes, perfectly! You have such wonderful daughters. Such fascinating conversation!"

Mama Elena sent Tita to the kitchen to get something for the guests. Pedro "happened" to be walking by at that moment and he offered his help. Tita rushed off to the kitchen without a word. His presence made her extremely uncomfortable. He followed her in, and she quickly sent him off with one of the trays of delicious snacks that had been waiting on the kitchen table.

She would never forget the moment their hands accidentally touched as they both slowly bent down to pick up the same tray.

That was when Pedro confessed his love.

"Señorita Tita, I would like to take advantage of this opportunity to be alone with you to tell you that I am deeply in love with you. I know this declaration is presumptuous, and that it's quite sudden, but it's so hard to get near you that I decided to tell you tonight. All I ask is that you tell me whether I can hope to win your love."

"I don't know what to say . . . give me time to think."

"No, no, I can't! I need an answer now: you don't have to think about love; you either feel it or you don't. I am a man of few words, but my word is my pledge. I swear that my love for you will last forever. What about you? Do you feel the same way about me?"

"Yes!"

Yes, a thousand times. From that night on she would love him forever. And now she had to give him up. It wasn't decent to desire your sister's future husband. She had to try to put him out of her mind somehow, so she could get to sleep. She started to eat the Christmas Roll Nacha had left out on her bureau, along with a glass of milk; this remedy had proven effective many times. Nacha, with all her experience, knew that for Tita there was no pain that wouldn't disappear if she ate a delicious Christmas Roll. But this time it didn't work. She felt no relief from the hollow sensation in her stomach. Just the opposite, a wave of nausea flowed over her. She realized that the hollow sensation was not hunger but an icy feeling of grief. She had to get rid of that terrible sensation of cold. First she put on a wool robe and a heavy cloak. The cold still gripped her. Then she put on felt slippers and another two shawls. No good. Finally she went to her sewing box and pulled out the bedspread she had started the day Pedro first spoke of marriage. A bedspread like that, a crocheted one, takes about a year to complete. Exactly the length of time Pedro and Tita had planned to wait before getting married. She decided to use the yarn, not to let it go to waste, and so she worked on the bedspread and wept furiously, weeping and working until dawn, and threw it over herself. It didn't help at all. Not that night, nor many others, for as long as she lived, could she free herself from that cold.

TO BE CONTINUED . . .

Next month's recipe:

Chabela Wedding Cake

CHAPTER TWO

FEBRUARY

Chabela Wedding Cake

INGREDIENTS:

175 grams refined granulated
  sugar
300 grams cake flour, sifted
  three times
17 eggs
grated peel of one lime

PREPARATION:

Place five egg yolks, four whole eggs, and the sugar in a large bowl. Beat until the mixture thickens and then add two more whole eggs; repeat, adding the remaining eggs two at a time until all the eggs have been added. To make the cake for Pedro and Rosaura's wedding, Tita and Nacha had to multiply this recipe by ten, since they were preparing a cake not for eighteen people but for 180. Therefore, they needed 170 eggs, which meant they had to arrange to have that number of good eggs on the same day.

To get that number of eggs together, they preserved all the eggs laid by the best hens for several weeks. This preserving technique had been employed on the ranch since time immemorial to ensure a supply of this nourishing and indispensable food throughout the winter. The best time to preserve eggs is August or September. The eggs must be very fresh. Nacha preferred to use only eggs laid the same day. The eggs are placed in a cask containing crumbled sheep fodder, allowed to cool, and then covered completely. This will keep the eggs fresh for months. If you want them to keep for more than a year, place the eggs in an earthenware crock and cover them with a ten-percent lime solution. Cover tightly to keep the air out and store in the wine cellar. Tita and Nacha had chosen to use the first method because they didn't need to keep the eggs fresh for that many months. They had placed the cask containing the preserved eggs between them under the kitchen table and were taking the eggs out of it as they put the cake together.

When she had beaten barely a hundred eggs, the phenomenal energy required for the task began to have a bad effect on Tita's mood. To reach the goal of 170 seemed unimaginable.

Tita beat the mixture while Nacha broke the eggs and added them to it. A fit of trembling shook Tita's body and she broke out in goose bumps when each new egg was broken. The egg whites reminded her of the testicles of the chickens they had castrated the month before. Roosters that are castrated and then fattened up are called capons. The family had decided to serve capons at Pedro and Rosaura's wedding because they would impress everyone with the quality of the dinner, as much for the amount of work required in their preparation as for the extraordinary flavor of the birds themselves.

As soon as the date of the wedding was set for the twelfth of January, they ordered two hundred roosters to be bought for castrating and fattening up.

This task fell to Tita and Nacha. Nacha because of

her experience and Tita as punishment for feigning a headache to avoid her sister Rosaura's engagement.

"I won't stand for disobedience," Mama Elena told her, "nor am I going to allow you to ruin your sister's wedding, with your acting like a victim. You're in charge of all the preparations starting now, and don't ever let me catch you with a single tear or even a long face, do you hear?"

Tita was trying to keep that warning in mind as she got set to castrate the first chicken. The castration is done by making an incision over the chicken's testicles, sticking your finger in to get a hold of them, and pulling them out. After that is done, the wound is sewn up and rubbed with fresh lard or chicken fat. Tita almost swooned when she stuck her finger in and grasped the testicles of the first chicken. Her hands were shaking and she was dripping sweat and her stomach was swooping like a kite on the wind. Mama Elena looked at her piercingly, and said:

"What's the matter? Why the shaking? Are we going to start having problems?" Tita raised her eyes and looked at her. She felt like screaming, Yes, she was having problems, when they had chosen something to be neutered, they'd made a mistake, they should have chosen her. At least then there would be some justification for not allowing her to marry and giving Rosaura her place beside the man she loved. Mama Elena read the look on her face and flew into a rage, giving Tita a tremendous slap that left her rolling in the dirt by the rooster, which had died from the bungled operation.

In a frenzy Tita beat, beat, beat the cake batter, as if

she wanted to complete her martyrdom once and for all. She had only to beat in two more eggs and the batter would be ready. The cake was the last thing to be done; everything else, all the food for a twenty-course meal and the appetizers that would precede it, was ready for the banquet. Only Tita, Nacha, and Mama Elena remained in the kitchen. Chencha, Gertrudis, and Rosaura were putting the finishing touches on the wedding dress. Nacha, with a loud sigh of relief, picked up the second to last egg to crack it into the bowl. Tita's shout stopped her.

"No!"

Tita stopped beating the cake and took the egg in her hand. The sound was quite clear, she could hear a baby chick peeping inside the shell. She held the egg closer to her ear and the peeping got louder. Mama Elena stopped what she was doing and addressed Tita in an authoritarian voice:

"What happened? Why did you scream?"

"Because there's a chicken inside this egg! Of course Nacha can't hear it, but I can."

"A chicken? Are you crazy? There has never been such a thing in a preserved egg!"

With two giant strides Mama Elena was next to Tita, grabbing the egg from her hand and cracking it open. Tita shut her eyes as tight as she could.

"Open your eyes and look at your chicken!"

Tita opened her eyes slowly. Surprised, she saw that what she had taken for a chicken was just an egg, and a fresh one at that.

"Listen to me, Tita. You are trying my patience. I

won't let you start acting crazy. This is the first and the last time for craziness! Or you will be sorry, I promise you that."

Tita never could explain what had happened to her that night, whether the sound she had heard was just fatigue or a hallucination, a product of her mind. At the time, her best course seemed to be to go back to beating the eggs, since she had no wish to test the limits of her mother's patience.

When the last two eggs have been beaten in, beat in the grated lime peel. When the mixture has thickened, stop beating and add the sifted flour, mixing it in a little at a time with a wooden spoon until it has all been incorporated. Finally, grease a pan with butter, dust with flour, and pour the batter into it. Bake for thirty minutes.

After spending three days preparing twenty different courses, Nacha was exhausted, and she could hardly wait for the cake to go in the oven so she could finally rest. Today Tita was not as good a helper as usual. Not that she made any complaints—under her mother's watchful eye she didn't dare—but when Mama Elena left the kitchen to go to bed, Tita let out a long sigh. Nacha gently took the spoon out of her hand and embraced her:

"Now we're alone in the kitchen, so go ahead and cry, my child, because I don't want them to see you crying tomorrow. Especially not Rosaura."

Nacha stopped Tita's stirring because she felt that Tita was on the verge of nervous collapse; though she didn't know the word for Tita's condition, she was wise enough to realize that Tita could not go on. Nor, in fact, could she. Rosaura and Nacha had never been close. Nacha was annoyed by Rosaura's picky eating, which had gone on since she was a child. She left her food untouched on her plate, or secretly fed it to Tequila, the father of Pulques, the ranch dog. Tita on the other hand had always been a good eater; she would eat anything. There was just one thing Tita didn't like: the soft-boiled eggs Mama Elena tried to make her eat. After Nacha had been put in charge of Tita's culinary education, she not only ate ordinary food, she also ate jumil bugs, maguey worms, crayfish, tepezcuintle pigs, armadillos, and other things that horrified Rosaura. That's how Nacha's dislike of Rosaura began, and the rivalry between the sisters was now culminating in this wedding between Rosaura and the man Tita loved. Rosaura wasn't sure, but she suspected that Pedro's love for Tita was never-ending. Nacha was on Tita's side, and she was doing everything she could to spare her pain. With her apron she dried the tears that were rolling down Tita's cheeks and said:

"Now, my child, we must finish the cake."

That took longer than it should have; the batter wouldn't thicken because Tita kept crying.

And so, arms around each other, Nacha and Tita wept until there were no more tears in Tita's eyes. Then she cried without tears, which is said to hurt even more, like dry labor; but at least she wasn't making the cake batter soggy, so they could go on to the next step, which is making the filling.

FOR THE FILLING:

150 grams apricot paste
150 grams granulated sugar

TO PREPARE THE FILLING:

Heat the apricot paste together with a little bit of water; after the mixture comes to a boil, strain it, preferably through a hair or flour sieve, but a coarser strainer can be used if you don't have either of those. Place the paste in a pan, add the sugar, and heat, stirring constantly, until the mixture forms a marmalade. Remove from the heat and allow to cool slightly before spreading it on the middle layer of the cake, which, of course, has previously been sliced into layers.

Luckily, Nacha and Tita had made several jars of preserves—apricot, fig, and camote with pineapple—the month before the wedding. Thanks to that, they were spared the task of making the marmalade filling the same day.

They often made enormous batches of jam, using whatever fruit was in season, which they cooked in a huge copper saucepan on the patio. The pan was set up over a fire, and they had to cover their arms with old sheets to stir the marmalade. This prevented the bubbles from boiling up and burning their skin.

The moment Tita opened the jar, the smell of apricots transported her to the afternoon they made the marmalade. Tita had come in from the kitchen garden, carrying the fruit in her skirt because she had forgotten a basket. She walked into the kitchen with her skirt held up in front of her and was startled to bump into Pedro. Pedro was heading out to get the carriage ready. They had to deliver some invitations in town, and since the head groom had not showed up at the ranch that day, the job had fallen upon Pedro. When Nacha saw him enter the kitchen, she left, practically at a run, on the pretext of cutting some epazote to add to the beans. Startled as she was, Tita dropped a few of the apricots. Pedro quickly came over to help her pick them up. Bending down, he could see the part of her leg that was exposed.

To prevent Pedro from looking at her leg, Tita let go of her skirt.

When she did, all the rest of the apricots rolled onto Pedro's head.

"Forgive me, Pedro. Did I hurt you?"

"Not as much as I have hurt you. Let me say that my intention . . ."

"I didn't ask for an explanation."

"You have to let me say a few words. . . ."

"I let you do that once, and all I got was lies. I don't want to hear any more. . . ."

With that Tita fled from the kitchen into the room where Chencha and Gertrudis were embroidering the sheet for the wedding night. It was a white silk sheet, and they were embroidering a delicate pattern in the center of it. This opening was designed to reveal only the bride's essential parts while allowing marital intimacy. How lucky they had been to obtain French silk at that time of political instability. The revolution made it impossible to travel in safety, which is why, if it hadn't been for a Chinaman who dealt in smuggled goods, it would have been impossible to obtain the material, since Mama Elena would never have allowed one of her daughters to risk traveling to the capital to buy the things for Rosaura's dress and trousseau. This Chinaman was a crafty fellow: he accepted notes issued by the revolutionary army in the North as payment for the merchandise he sold in the capital, even though the notes were worthless and not negotiable there. Naturally when he took these notes in payment, it was at a fraction of their value, but then he took them to the North, where they were worth their full value, and bought goods with them.

In the North, he accepted the notes issued in the capital, at low value, of course, and so he spent the entire revolution, until he wound up a millionaire. But the important thing is that thanks to him Rosaura would be able to enjoy the finest, most exquisite fabric on her wedding night.

Tita stood as if in a trance, staring at the whiteness of the sheet; only for a few seconds, but long enough to cause a sort of blindness. Wherever she looked she saw the color white. When she looked at Rosaura, who was writing out some invitations, she saw only a snowy ghost. But she showed nothing, and no one noticed her condition.

She didn't want another rebuke from Mama Elena. When the Lobos arrived to give Rosaura her wedding present, Tita tried to sharpen her senses to figure out who was greeting her, since to her they looked like porcelain ghosts covered by white sheets. Fortunately Paquita's shrill voice gave Tita the solution to her problem and she was able to greet them without much of a problem.

Later, when she accompanied the Lobos to the entrance of the ranch, she noted that she had never seen such a night before; to her it was all a blinding whiteness.

Now she was afraid the same thing would happen again, for she was unable to concentrate on making the icing for the cake, no matter how hard she tried. The whiteness of the granulated sugar frightened her. She felt powerless against it, feeling that at any moment the white color might seize her mind, dragging along those snow-white images from her childhood, May-time images of being taken all in white, to offer white flowers to the Virgin. She entered the church in a row of girls all dressed in white and approached the altar, which was covered with white candles and flowers, illuminated by a heavenly white light streaming through the stained-glass window of the white church. Never had she entered that church, not once, without dreaming of the day she would enter it on the arm of a man. She had to block out not just this thought but all the memories that caused her so much pain: she had to finish the frosting for her sister's wedding cake. Making a supreme effort, she began to prepare it.

FOR THE FONDANT ICING:

800 grams granulated sugar
60 drops of lime juice plus enough water to dissolve the sugar

TO PREPARE THE FONDANT:

Combine the sugar and water in a pan and heat, stirring constantly, until the mixture comes to a boil. Strain into another pan and return to the heat; add the lime juice and cook until it reaches the soft-ball stage, wiping the edge of the pan with a damp cloth periodically to prevent the sugar from crystallizing. When the mixture reaches that stage, pour it into a damp pan, sprinkle with water, and allow to cool slightly.

After it cools, beat with a wooden spoon until creamy.

To ice the cake, add a tablespoon of milk to the fondant, heat until it softens, add a drop of red food color, and frost only the top part of the cake with the fondant icing.

Nacha realized something was wrong with Tita when she asked if Nacha was going to add the red food color to the icing.

"Child, I've already added it, can't you see how pink it is?"

"No . . ."

"Go to bed, child, I'll finish the meringue icing. Only the pan knows how the boiling soup feels, but I know how you feel, so stop crying, you're getting the meringue watery, and it won't set up properly—go now, go."

Nacha covered Tita with kisses and pushed her out of the kitchen. Tita didn't explain the reason for those new tears, but now they had been shed, and they had changed the consistency of the meringue. Now it would be twice as hard to get it to form peaks. All that mattered was to finish the meringue as fast as she could so she could go to sleep. The meringue icing requires ten egg whites and five hundred grams of sugar, which are beaten together until they reach the coarse-thread stage.

When she finished beating the meringue, it occurred to Nacha to lick some of the icing off her finger to see if Tita's tears had affected the flavor. No, the flavor did not seem to have been affected; yet without knowing why, Nacha was suddenly overcome with an intense longing.

One after another, she thought back on all the wedding banquets she had prepared for the De la Garza family, ever cherishing the illusion that the next wedding would be her own. At eighty-five, there was no longer much point in crying, lamenting the wedding banquet she'd been waiting for that had never come, or the wedding she had never had, even though she had had a fiancé. Oh yes, she had! But the mama of Mama Elena had sent him packing. Since then, all she could do was enjoy other people's weddings, as she had been doing for years without grumbling. So why was she complaining now? There must be some joke in all this, but she couldn't find it. She frosted the cake with the meringue icing as well as she could and went to her room, a terrible aching in her heart. She cried all night, and the next morning she didn't have the strength to help with the wedding.

Tita would have given anything to change places with Nacha. Tita not only had to attend the wedding ceremony, despite her feelings, she also had to make sure her face did not reveal the slightest emotion. She thought she could manage it, as long as her eyes didn't meet Pedro's. That would shatter her pretense of calm and composure.

She was aware that she, not her sister Rosaura, was the center of attention. The wedding guests were not just performing a social act, they wanted to observe her suffering; but she wouldn't give them that satisfaction. No. She heard, as she passed, the whispers in the church, and she felt each comment like a stab in her back.

"Have you seen Tita? The poor thing, her sister is going to marry her sweetheart! I saw them one day in the plaza in the village, holding hands. They looked so happy."

"You don't say! And Paquita says that at High Mass one day she saw Pedro passing Tita a love letter, perfumed and everything!"

"They say they're going to live in the same house! If I were Mama Elena, I wouldn't allow it!"

"I don't see how she can. Look how much gossip there is already!"

Tita didn't care for these comments at all. She was not meant for the loser's role. She would put on a triumphant expression. Like a great actress, she played her role with dignity, trying to think about anything but the wedding march and the priest's words, the knot and the rings.

Her mind bore her back to one day when she was nine, when she had played hooky from school with some boys from the village. She wasn't supposed to play with boys, but she was sick of her sisters' games. They went to the Rio Grande, to see who could swim across it the fastest. She had been the winner—how proud she had been.

One quiet Sunday in the village she had scored another of her great triumphs. She was fourteen. She and her sisters were taking a carriage ride when some boys set off a firecracker. The frightened horses bolted. When they came to the edge of the village, they ran wild and the driver could not control them.

Tita shoved him aside and brought the four horses back under control singlehandedly. When four men from the village galloped up to rescue the sisters, they were amazed at Tita's daring feat.

The villagers gave her a heroine's reception.

She kept her mind on these and other memories like them in order to maintain a little contented-cat smile throughout the ceremony, until it was kissing time and she had to congratulate her sister. Pedro, who was standing with Rosaura, said to Tita:

"And me, aren't you going to congratulate me?"

"Yes, of course. I hope you will be very happy."

Pedro, holding her much closer than convention allowed, took advantage of this unique opportunity to whisper in Tita's ear:

"I am sure I will be, since through this marriage I have gained what I really wanted: the chance to be near you, the woman I really love. . . ."

For Tita, these words were like a fresh breeze fanning embers that had been about to die. She had had to hide her feelings for so many months that her expression now changed dramatically, and her relief and happiness were obvious. It was as if all her inner joy, which had nearly been extinguished, had suddenly been rekindled by Pedro's warm breath upon her neck, the hot touch of his hands upon her back, his chest pressed impulsively against her breasts. . . . She could have stayed in his arms forever, but a look from her mother made her pull away in a hurry. Mama Elena came over to Tita:

"What did Pedro say to you?"

"Nothing, Mami."

"Don't try to trick me, I'm wise to your games. I've been through them before. Don't play innocent with me. You'll be sorry if I ever catch you around Pedro again."

After Mama Elena's threats, Tita tried to keep as much distance as she could between herself and Pedro.

But it was impossible for her to wipe that smile of sheer satisfaction off her face. The wedding now had an entirely new significance for her.

Seeing Pedro and Rosaura go from table to table chatting with the guests, watching them dance the waltz or cut the cake no longer bothered Tita a bit. She knew now that it was true: Pedro loved her. It was killing her waiting for the dinner to end to run tell Nacha everything. She could hardly wait until everyone was done with the cake so she could leave the table. Carreno's manual of etiquette said she couldn't leave until then, so she kept her head in the clouds and gobbled down her piece of cake. She was so wrapped up in her thoughts that she didn't notice that all around her something very strange was taking place. The moment they took their first bite of the cake, everyone was flooded with a great wave of longing. Even Pedro, usually so proper, was having trouble holding back his tears. Mama Elena, who hadn't shed a single tear over her husband's death, was sobbing silently. But the weeping was just the first symptom of a strange intoxication—an acute attack of pain and frustration—that seized the guests and scattered them across the patio and the grounds and in the bathrooms, all of them wailing over lost love. Everyone there, every last person, fell under this spell, and not very many of them made it to the bathrooms in time—those who didn't joined the collective vomiting that was going on all over the patio. Only one person escaped: the cake had no effect on Tita. The minute she finished eating it, she left the party. She urgently wanted to tell Nacha that she had been right in saying Pedro loved only her. Envisioning the happiness that would spread across Nacha's face, she didn't notice that with every step the scenes of misery around her, pathetic and horrifying, were growing worse.

Rosaura, retching, abandoned her place of honor.

She struggled to control her nausea, but it was too much for her! Her only concern was to keep her wedding dress from being fouled by the degradations of her relatives and friends; but as she crossed the patio she slipped and every inch of her dress ended up coated with vomit. She was swept away in a raging rotting river for several yards; then she couldn't hold back anymore, and she spewed out great noisy mouthfuls of vomit, like an erupting volcano, right before Pedro's horrified eyes. Rosaura complained bitterly about the way her wedding had been ruined, and no power on earth could convince her that Tita had not added something to the cake.

She spent the whole night moaning, in such torment that the thought of the sheets that had taken so long to embroider was driven completely out of her mind. Pedro quickly proposed they leave the consummation of the nuptials for another night. But it was months before Pedro finally found himself obliged to do it, and then only because Rosaura dared to point out to him that she was now completely recovered. That night, realizing that he wouldn't be able to ignore his conjugal duty forever, Pedro knelt by the bed, on which the nuptial sheet was spread, and offered up this prayer:

"Lord, this is not lust or lewdness but to make a child to serve you."

Tita never dreamed that it had taken so long for the ill-fated marriage to be consummated. It didn't make any difference to her whether it was after the wedding or any other day.

Tita was more worried about saving her skin than about anything else. The night of the wedding reception she had gotten a tremendous hiding from Mama Elena, like no beating before or since. She spent two weeks in bed recovering from her bruises. What motivated such a monstrous punishment was Mama Elena's conviction that Tita, in league with Nacha, had deliberately ruined Rosaura's wedding by mixing an emetic into the cake. Tita was never able to convince her that she had only added one extra ingredient to the cake, the tears she had shed while preparing it. Nor could Nacha testify on her behalf: on the day of the wedding, when Tita went looking for her, she found Nacha lying dead, her eyes wide open, medicinal leaves upon her temples, a picture of her fiancé clutched in her hands.

TO BE CONTINUED . . .

Next month's recipe:

Quail in Rose Petal Sauce

CHAPTER THREE

March

Quail in Rose Petal
Sauce

INGREDIENTS:

12 roses, preferably red
12 chestnuts
2 teaspoons butter
2 teaspoons cornstarch
2 drops attar of roses
2 tablespoons anise
2 tablespoons honey
2 cloves garlic
6 quail
1 pitaya

PREPARATION:

Remove the petals carefully from the roses, trying not to prick your fingers, for not only are the little wounds painful but the petals could soak up blood that might alter the flavor of the dish and even produce dangerous chemical reactions.

How could Tita remember such a thing, shaken as she was to get a bouquet of roses, and from Pedro besides. It was the first deep emotion she had felt since her sister's wedding, when she had heard Pedro confirm his love, trying to hide it from everyone's prying eyes. Mama Elena's eyes were as sharp as ever and she knew what would happen if Pedro and Tita ever got the chance to be alone. As a result, she had resorted to staging the most amazing acts of prestidigitation, always managing to pull off her trick of keeping them out of each other's sight and reach, until today. She had let one little thing slip past her: with Nacha dead, Tita was the best qualified of all the women in the house to fill the vacant post in the kitchen, and in there flavors, smells, textures, and the effects they could have were beyond Mama Elena's iron command.

Tita was the last link in a chain of cooks who had been passing culinary secrets from generation to generation since ancient times, and she was considered the finest exponent of the marvelous art of cooking. Naming her official ranch cook was a popular decision with everyone. Tita was pleased to receive the post, in spite of the sorrow she felt at losing Nacha.

Her unfortunate death had left Tita in a very deep depression. With Nacha dead she was completely alone. It was as if her real mother had died. To help her get over it, Pedro thought it would be nice to bring her a bouquet of roses to celebrate her first year as ranch cook. But Rosaura—who was expecting her first child—did not agree, and when she saw him walk in carrying a bouquet for Tita, instead of her, she burst into tears and ran from the room.

With just a look Mama Elena sent Tita away to get rid of the roses. Now, too late, Pedro realized his foolhardiness. Again with a look, Mama Elena informed him there was still time to repair the damage. Such a look it was that he excused himself and went off to look for Rosaura. Tita clasped the roses to her chest so tightly that when she got to the kitchen, the roses, which had been mostly pink, had turned quite red from the blood that was flowing from Tita's hands and breasts. She had to think fast what to do with them. They were beautiful. She couldn't just throw them in the trash; in the first place, she'd never been given flowers before, and second, they were from Pedro. All at once she seemed to hear Nacha's voice dictating a recipe, a prehispanic recipe involving rose petals. Tita had nearly forgotten it because it called for pheasants, which they didn't raise on the ranch.

The one bird they did have was quail. She decided to revise the recipe slightly, just so she could use the flowers.

Without a second thought, she went to the patio to catch the quail. When she had caught six, she carried them into the kitchen and got ready to kill them—which would be hard, having fed and cared for them for so long.

With a deep breath, she took hold of the first one and twisted its neck, as she had seen Nacha do so often, but she used too little force to kill the poor quail, which went running pitifully around the kitchen, its head hanging to one side. She was horrified! She realized that you can't be weak when it comes to killing: you have to be strong or it just causes more sorrow. It occurred to her that she could use her mother's strength right now. Mama Elena was merciless, killing with a single blow. But then again not always. For Tita she had made an exception; she had been killing her a little at a time since she was a child, and she still hadn't quite finished her off. Pedro and Rosaura's marriage had left Tita broken in both heart and in mind, like the quail. To spare the quail the pain she felt, Tita moved sharply and decisively, finishing him off as an act of mercy. With the others it was easier. She just pretended that each quail had a soft-boiled egg stuck in its crop and that she was delivering it from this suffering, mercifully, by giving its neck a good twist. As a child she would have chosen death over those soft-boiled eggs she was made to eat. Mama Elena forced them on her. She would feel her throat tighten, so tight she couldn't swallow any kind of food, until her mother gave her a smack that miraculously loosened the knot in her throat; then the egg slid down without any problem. Feeling calmer, she had no difficulty in completing the next steps.

So skillful was she that it seemed Nacha herself was in Tita's body doing all those things: dry-plucking the birds, removing the viscera, getting them ready for frying.

After the quail are plucked and dressed, their feet are pulled together and tied so that the bird keeps a nice shape after being browned in butter and sprinkled with salt and pepper to taste.

The quail must be dry-plucked because putting them in boiling water affects their flavor. That is just one of many cooking secrets that can only be learned through practice. Ever since she had burned her hands on the griddle, Rosaura wanted nothing to do with any kind of culinary activity, so she was ignorant of that and many other gastronomical secrets. But whether she did it to impress her husband Pedro or to compete with Tita in her own territory—who can say?—there was one day when Rosaura did attempt to cook. When Tita tried nicely to give her some advice, Rosaura became irritated and asked Tita to leave her alone in the kitchen.

The rice was obviously scorched, the meat dried out, the dessert burnt. But no one at the table dared display the tiniest hint of displeasure, not after Mama Elena had pointedly remarked:

"As the first meal that Rosaura has cooked it isn't bad. Don't you agree, Pedro?"

Making a real effort not to insult his wife, Pedro replied:

"No, for her first time, it's not too bad."

Of course, that afternoon the entire family felt sick to their stomachs.

That had been a tragedy, but nothing like the one that shook the ranch this time. Tita's blood and the roses from Pedro proved quite an explosive combination.

Everyone was a little tense as they sat down at the table, but that's as far as it went until the quail were served. It wasn't enough he'd made his wife jealous earlier, for when Pedro tasted his first mouthful, he couldn't help closing his eyes in voluptuous delight and exclaiming:

"It is a dish for the gods!"

Mama Elena knew that the quail was exquisite; nonetheless, Pedro's remark did not sit well with her, and she replied:

"It's too salty."

Rosaura, saying she was feeling sick and getting nauseous, barely took three bites. But something strange was happening to Gertrudis.

On her the food seemed to act as an aphrodisiac; she began to feel an intense heat pulsing through her limbs. An itch in the center of her body kept her from sitting properly in her chair. She began to sweat, imagining herself on horseback with her arms clasped around one of Pancho Villa's men: the one she had seen in the village plaza the week before, smelling of sweat and mud, of dawns that brought uncertainty and danger, smelling of

life and of death. She was on her way to market in
Piedras Negras with Chencha, the servant, when she saw
him coming down the main street, riding in front of the
others, obviously the captain of the troop. Their eyes
met and what she saw in his made her tremble. She saw
all the nights he'd spent staring into the fire and longing
to have a woman beside him, a woman he could kiss, a
woman he could hold in his arms, a woman like her. She
got out her handkerchief and tried to wipe these sinful
thoughts from her mind as she wiped away the sweat.

But it was no use, something strange had happened
to her. She turned to Tita for help, but Tita wasn't there,
even though her body was sitting up quite properly in
her chair; there wasn't the slightest sign of life in her
eyes. It was as if a strange alchemical process had dissolved her entire being in the rose petal sauce, in the
tender flesh of the quails, in the wine, in every one of the
meal's aromas. That was the way she entered Pedro's
body, hot, voluptuous, perfumed, totally sensuous.

With that meal it seemed they had discovered a new
system of communication, in which Tita was the trans-
mitter, Pedro the receiver, and poor Gertrudis the medium, the conducting body through which the singular
sexual message was passed.

Pedro didn't offer any resistance. He let Tita penetrate to the farthest corners of his being, and all the
while they couldn't take their eyes off each other. He
said:

"Thank you, I have never had anything so exquisite."

It truly is a delicious dish. The roses give it an extremely delicate flavor.

After the petals are removed from the roses, they are

ground with the anise in a mortar. Separately, brown the chestnuts in a pan, remove the peels, and cook them in water. Then, puree them. Mince the garlic and brown slightly in butter; when it is transparent, add it to the chestnut puree, along with the honey, the ground pitaya, and the rose petals, and salt to taste. To thicken the sauce slightly, you may add two teaspoons of cornstarch. Last, strain through a fine sieve and add no more than two drops of attar of roses, since otherwise it might have too strong a flavor and smell. As soon as the seasoning has been added, remove the sauce from the heat. The quail should be immersed in this sauce for ten minutes to infuse them with the flavor, and then removed.

The smell of attar of roses is so penetrating that the mortar used to grind the petals will smell like roses for several days.

The job of washing that and all the other kitchen utensils fell to Gertrudis. She washed them after each meal, out on the patio, so she could throw the scraps left in the pans to the animals. Since some of the utensils were large, it was also easier to wash them in the wash basin. But the day they had the quail, she asked Tita to do the washing up for her. Gertrudis was really stricken; her whole body was dripping with sweat. Her sweat was pink, and it smelled like roses, a lovely strong smell. In desperate need of a shower, she ran to get it ready.

Behind the patio by the stable and the corn crib, Mama Elena had had a primitive shower rigged up. It was a small room made of planks nailed together, except that between one board and the next, there were such big cracks that it was easy to see the person who was taking the shower. Still, it was the first shower of any

kind that had ever been seen in the village. A cousin of
Mama Elena's who lived in San Antonio, Texas, had in-
vented it. It had a thirty-gallon tank that was six feet
high: first, you filled the tank with water, then you got a
shower using gravity. It was hard work carrying buckets
of water up the wooden ladder, but it was delightful
afterward just to open the tap and feel the water run over
your whole body in a steady stream, not doled out the
way it was if you bathed using gourds full of water. Years
later some gringos got this invention from Mama Elena's
cousin for a song and made a few improvements. They
made thousands of showers that used pipes, so you didn't
have to do all that damn filling.

If Gertrudis had only known! The poor thing
climbed up and down ten times, carrying buckets of water. It was brutal exercise, which made the heat that
burned her body grow more and more intense, until she
nearly fainted.

The only thing that kept her going was the image of
the refreshing shower ahead of her, but unfortunately
she was never able to enjoy it, because the drops that fell
from the shower never made it to her body: they evapo-
rated before they reached her. Her body was giving off
so much heat that the wooden walls began to split and
burst into flame. Terrified, she thought she would be
burnt to death, and she ran out of the little enclosure just
as she was, completely naked.

By then the scent of roses given off by her body had
traveled a long, long way. All the way to town, where
the rebel forces and the federal troops were engaged in a
fierce battle. One man stood head and shoulders above

the others for his valor; it was the rebel who Gertrudis had seen in the plaza in Piedras Negras the week before.

A pink cloud floated toward him, wrapped itself around him, and made him set out at a gallop toward Mama Elena's ranch. Juan—for that was the soldier's name—abandoned the field of battle, leaving an enemy soldier not quite dead, without knowing why he did so. A higher power was controlling his actions. He was moved by a powerful urge to arrive as quickly as possible at a meeting with someone unknown in some undetermined place. But it wasn't hard to find. The aroma from Gertrudis' body guided him. He got there just in time to find her racing through the field. Then he knew why he'd been drawn there. This woman desperately needed a man to quench the red-hot fire that was raging inside her.

A man equal to loving someone who needed love as much as she did, a man like him.

Gertrudis stopped running when she saw him riding toward her. Naked as she was, with her loosened hair falling to her waist, luminous, glowing with energy, she might have been an angel and devil in one woman. The delicacy of her face, the perfection of her pure virginal body contrasted with the passion, the lust, that leapt from her eyes, from her every pore. These things, and the sexual desire Juan had contained for so long while he was fighting in the mountains, made for a spectacular encounter.

Without slowing his gallop, so as not to waste a moment, he leaned over, put his arm around her waist, and lifted her onto the horse in front of him, face to face, and carried her away. The horse, which seemed to be obeying higher orders too, kept galloping as if it already knew their ultimate destination, even though Juan had thrown the reins aside and was passionately kissing and embracing Gertrudis. The movement of the horse combined with the movement of their bodies as they made love for the first time, at a gallop and with a great deal of difficulty.

They were going so fast that the escort following Juan never caught up with him. Liars tell half-truths and he told everyone that during the battle the captain had suddenly gone crazy and deserted the army.

That is the way history gets written, distorted by eyewitness accounts that don't really match the reality. Tita saw the incident from a completely different perspective than the rebel soldiers. She watched the whole thing from the patio as she was washing the dishes. She didn't miss a thing in spite of the rosy clouds of steam and the flames shooting out of the bathroom, which made it hard for her to see. Pedro, too, was lucky enough to witness the spectacle, since he was just leaving the patio on his bicycle to go for a ride.

Like silent spectators to a movie, Pedro and Tita began to cry watching the stars act out the love that was denied to them. There was a moment, one brief instant, when Pedro could have changed the course of their story. Taking Tita's hand in his, he began to talk to her:
—Tita . . . But that was all. There was no time to finish. He was forced back to grim reality. He had heard Mama Elena's shout, asking what was going on out on the patio. If Pedro had asked Tita to run away with him, she wouldn't have hesitated for a moment, but he didn't;

instead, he quickly hopped onto his bicycle and furiously pedaled away. He couldn't get the image of Gertrudis out of his mind, Gertrudis running through the field— completely naked. He must have been hypnotized by her ample breasts swinging from side to side. He'd never seen a naked woman before. During his relations with Rosaura, he'd never had any desire to see her body or caress it. They always used the nuptial sheet, which re- vealed only the necessary parts of his wife's body. When he was done, he would leave the bedroom before she became uncovered. But it was different with Tita, and he longed to gaze at her that way, without any clothes on.

He wanted to study, examine, investigate every last inch of skin on her lovely, monumental body. Surely, she'd look like Gertrudis; they weren't sisters for noth- ing.

The only part of Tita's body that he knew very well, other than her face and hands, was the little round bit of leg he'd once managed to glimpse. The memory of it tortured him each night. How he longed to place his hand over that little patch of skin, and then all over her, as he had seen the man who took Gertrudis do: madly, passionately, lustfully!

Tita, for her part, was trying to shout to Pedro to wait for her, to take her away with him, far away where they'd be allowed to love each other, where there were no rules to keep them apart, where there was no Mama —but not a single sound came out of her mouth. The words formed a lump in her throat and were choked one after another as they tried to escape.

She felt so lost and lonely. One last chile in walnut sauce left on the platter after a fancy dinner couldn't feel any worse than she did. How many times had she eaten one of those treats, standing by herself in the kitchen, rather than let it be thrown away. When nobody eats the last chile on the plate, it's usually because none of them wants to look like a glutton, so even though they'd really like to devour it, they don't have the nerve to take it. It was as if they were rejecting that stuffed pepper, which contains every imaginable flavor; sweet as candied citron, juicy as a pomegranate, with the bit of pepper and the subtlety of walnuts, that marvelous chile in walnut sauce. Within it lies the secret of love, but it will never be penetrated, and all because it wouldn't be proper.

Damn good manners! Damn Carreno's etiquette manual! He should be punished, his body made to fade away a bit at a time, forever. Damn Pedro, so decent, so proper, so manly, so . . . wonderful.

Had Tita known how soon she would taste physical love, she wouldn't have felt quite so hopeless.

Mama Elena's second shout shook her out of her brooding and forced her to come up with an answer fast. She didn't know what to tell her mama first, if she should tell her that the far end of the patio was on fire, or that Gertrudis had run off with one of Villa's men, on horseback . . . naked.

She settled on a version in which the Federal troops, which Tita hated, had swooped down on the ranch, set fire to the bathroom, and kidnapped Gertrudis. Mama Elena swallowed the whole thing; she was so sad it made her sick—but what nearly killed her was when she got the story from Father Ignacio, the parish priest—and who knew how he found out about it—that the next week Gertrudis was working in a brothel on the border.

Mama Elena burned Gertrudis' birth certificate and all of her pictures and said she didn't want to hear her name mentioned ever again.

Neither the fire nor the passage of time has been able to eliminate a strong smell of roses that lingers in the spot where the shower stood, which now is a parking lot for an apartment building. Nor could they efface the images that lingered in Pedro and Tita's minds, marking them forever. Ever after, quail in rose sauce became a silent reminder of this fascinating experience.

Each year Tita prepared it in tribute to her sister's liberation and she always took special care in arranging the garnish.

The quail are placed on a platter, the sauce is poured over them, and they are garnished with a single perfect rose in the center and rose petals scattered around the outside; or the quail can be served individually, on separate plates instead of a platter. That's how Tita liked to do it, because then there was no chance of the garnish sliding off-center when it was served, and that's what she specified in the cookbook she started writing that night, after crocheting a big section of bedspread, as she did every night. As she worked, images of Gertrudis went around and around in her head: Gertrudis running through the field, and what she imagined had happened later, after her sister had disappeared from sight. Needless to say, her imagination was limited there by her lack of experience.

She wondered if Gertrudis had any clothes on now, or if she was still . . . naked! She worried that Gertrudis was cold, as cold as she was, but then she decided, no, she wasn't. Most likely she was near a fire,

in the arms of her man, and that would surely warm
her.

All of a sudden she had a thought that made her run
outside to look at the stars. Having felt it with her own
body, she knew a look could start a fire.

Even to set the sun itself ablaze. What then would
happen if Gertrudis looked up at a star? Surely the heat
from her body, which was inflamed by love, would travel
with that gaze across an infinite distance, with no loss of
energy, until it landed on the star she was watching.
Those huge stars have lasted for millions of years by
taking care never to absorb any of the fiery rays lovers all
over the world send up at them night after night. To
avoid that, the star generates so much heat inside itself
that it shatters the rays into a thousand pieces. Any look
it receives is immediately repulsed, reflected back onto
the earth, like a trick done with mirrors. That is the
reason the stars shine so brightly at night. Tita therefore
began to hope that if she could find the one star—
among all the stars in the sky—that her sister was watching right this minute, it might reflect a little leftover heat
onto her.

That was her dream, but the longer she scanned the
stars in the sky, one by one, the less she felt the tiniest
bit of warmth—just the opposite happened. Shivering,
she went back to bed, convinced that Gertrudis was
sound asleep, her eyes shut tight and that's why the experiment hadn't worked. So, pulling up the bedspread,
which by then had to be folded in thirds, she looked
over the recipe she had written to see if she had forgotten anything. And added: "Today while we were eating
this dish, Gertrudis ran away. . . ."

TO BE CONTINUED . . .

Next month's recipe:

Turkey Mole with Almonds and Sesame Seeds

CHAPTER FOUR

APRIL

*Turkey Mole
with Almonds and
Sesame Seeds*

INGREDIENTS:

1/4 chile mulato
3 chiles pasillas
3 chiles anchos
a handful of almonds
a handful of sesame seeds
turkey stock
a hard roll (¹/₃ concha loaf)
peanuts
1/2 onion
wine
2 squares of chocolate
anise
lard
cloves
cinnamon
pepper
sugar
seeds from the chiles
5 cloves garlic

PREPARATION:

Two days after killing the turkey, clean it and cook with salt. Turkey meat can be delicious, even exquisite, if the turkey has been fattened up properly. This can be accomplished by keeping the birds in clean pens with plenty of corn and water.

Fifteen days before the turkey is to be killed, begin feeding it small walnuts. Start with one the first day, the next day put two in its beak, and keep increasing the number this way until the night before it's to be killed, regardless of how much corn it eats voluntarily during this period.

Tita took care to feed the turkeys properly; she wanted the feast to go well, for the ranch was celebrating an important event: the baptism of her nephew, first son of Pedro and Rosaura. This event warranted a grand meal with mole. She had had a special set of earthenware dishes made for the occasion with the name *Roberto* on them, for that is what they had named the beautiful baby, on whom all the family and friends were lavishing gifts and attention. Especially Tita who, contrary to what she had expected, felt an immense tenderness toward the boy, completely overlooking the fact that he was the product of her sister's marriage to Pedro, the love of her life.

She was really excited as she started to prepare the mole the day before the baptism. Pedro, hearing her from the living room, experienced a sensation that was new to him. The sound of the pans bumping against each other, the smell of the almonds browning in the griddle, the sound of Tita's melodious voice, singing as she cooked, had kindled his sexual feelings. Just as lovers know the time for intimate relations is approaching from the closeness and smell of their beloved, or from the caresses exchanged in previous love play, so Pedro knew from those sounds and smells, especially the smell of browning sesame seeds, that there was a real culinary pleasure to come.

The almond and sesame seeds are toasted in a griddle. The chiles anchos, with their membranes removed, are also toasted—lightly, so they don't get bitter. This must be done in a separate frying pan, since a little lard is used. Afterward the toasted chiles are ground on a stone along with the almonds and sesame seeds.

Tita, on her knees, was bent over the grinding stone, moving in a slow regular rhythm, grinding the almonds and sesame seeds.

Under her blouse, her breasts moved freely, since she never wore a brassiere. Drops of sweat formed on her neck and ran down into the crease between her firm round breasts.

Pedro couldn't resist the smells from the kitchen and was heading toward them. But he stopped stock-still in the doorway, transfixed by the sight of Tita in that erotic posture.

Tita looked up without stopping her grinding and her eyes met Pedro's. At once their passionate glances fused so perfectly that whoever saw them would have seen but a single look, a single rhythmic and sensual motion, a single trembling breath, a single desire.

They stayed in this amorous ecstasy until Pedro lowered his eyes and stared steadily at Tita's breasts. She stopped grinding, straightened up, and proudly lifted her chest so Pedro could see it better. His scrutiny changed their relationship forever. After that penetrating look that saw through clothes, nothing would ever be the same. Tita knew through her own flesh how fire transforms the elements, how a lump of corn flour is changed into a tortilla, how a soul that hasn't been warmed by the fire of love is lifeless, like a useless ball of corn flour. In a few moments' time, Pedro had transformed Tita's breasts from chaste to experienced flesh, without even touching them.

If it hadn't been for Chencha walking in, back from buying some chiles anchos, who knows what would have happened between Pedro and Tita; perhaps Pedro would have ended up tirelessly caressing the breasts Tita offered him, but unfortunately that was not to be. Pedro pretended he'd come in for a glass of lime water with sage, quickly got it, and left the kitchen.

With shaking hands, Tita tried to go on preparing the mole as if nothing had happened.

When the almonds and sesame seeds have been thoroughly ground, mix them with the stock in which the turkey was cooked and add salt to taste. Grind the cloves, cinnamon, anise, and pepper, in a mortar, adding the roll last, after frying it in lard with chopped onion and garlic.

Next combine this mixture with the wine and blend well.

While she was grinding the spices, Chencha tried in vain to capture Tita's interest. But as much as she exaggerated the events she had witnessed in the plaza, describing in bloody detail the violent battles that had taken place in the village, Tita showed no more than a flicker of interest.

Today she couldn't keep her mind on anything other than the emotions she had just experienced. Besides, Tita knew perfectly well what Chencha was up to with these stories. Since she wasn't a girl to be frightened by stories of La Llorona, the witch who sucks little children's blood, or the boogeyman, or other scary stories, Chencha was trying to frighten her with stories of hangings, shootings, dismemberments, decapitations, and even sacrifices in which the victim's heart was cut out—in the heat of battle! On some other occasion she might have enjoyed getting carried away by Chencha's ridiculous story, and wound up believing her lies, even the one where Pancho Villa removes his enemies' bloody hearts so he can devour them, but not today.

Pedro's look had revived her faith in his love for her. For months she'd been tormented by the thought that

Pedro had lied to her on his wedding day, that he'd told her he loved her just so she wouldn't suffer, or that as time went on, he really had grown to love Rosaura. These doubts started when he suddenly, inexplicably, stopped raving about her cooking. Crushed, Tita took elaborate pains to cook better meals each day. In despair, at night—after she had knit a little section of bedspread, of course—she would invent new recipes, hoping to repair the connection that flowed between them through the food she prepared. Her finest recipes date from this period of suffering.

Just as a poet plays with words, Tita juggled ingredients and quantities at will, obtaining phenomenal results, and all for nothing: her best efforts were in vain. She couldn't drag a single word of appreciation out of Pedro's mouth. What she didn't know was that Mama Elena had "asked" Pedro to stop praising the meals, on the grounds that it made Rosaura feel insecure, when she was fat and misshapen because of her pregnancy, to have to listen to him compliment Tita in the guise of praising the delicious food she cooked.

How alone Tita felt during this period. How she missed Nacha! She hated them all, including Pedro. She was convinced she would never love anyone again as long as she lived. But it all melted away when she held Rosaura's son in her hands.

It had been a cold March morning. She was in the henhouse gathering the just-laid eggs to fix them for breakfast. Some of the eggs were still warm, so she put them in her blouse, next to her skin, to relieve her constant chill, which had gradually been getting worse. She got up before everyone else as usual.

But today she'd gotten up a half hour earlier than usual, to pack a suitcase with Gertrudis' clothes. Nicholas was making a trip to round up some cattle, and she planned to ask him to please take the suitcase to her sister. Of course, she had to hide all this from her mother. Tita wanted to send the clothes because she couldn't get the idea that Gertrudis was still naked out of her head. Not, of course, because of her sister's work in a bordertown brothel; rather, because Tita knew she hadn't taken any clothes with her.

She thrust at Nicholas the suitcase of clothes and an envelope bearing the address of the den where he might find Gertrudis, and she went back to her chores.

Soon she heard Pedro getting the carriage ready. Strange that he was doing that so early. But she saw from the sunlight that it was already late, that packing up some of Gertrudis' past along with her clothes, had taken longer than she had imagined. It hadn't been easy to fit into the suitcase the day the three of them made their First Communion. The veil, the prayerbook, the photo taken outside the church all fit in pretty well, but not the taste of the tamales and atole Nacha had made, which they had eaten afterward with their friends and families. The little colored apricot pits had gone in, but not their laughter when they played with them in the schoolyard, nor Jovita their teacher, the swing, the smell of her bedroom or of freshly whipped chocolate. Luckily, Mama Elena's scoldings and spankings hadn't fit in either; Tita had slammed the suitcase shut before they could sneak in.

Just as she got to the patio, Pedro began calling her desperately. He had to go to Eagle Pass for Dr. Brown, the family doctor, and he hadn't been able to find her anywhere. Rosaura had felt the first pains of labor.

Pedro asked Tita to please take care of her while he was gone.

Tita was the only one who could do it. No one else was left in the house. Mama Elena and Chencha had gone to the market to buy supplies for the baby, who was due any minute; they didn't want to lack any of the things that are indispensable at such a time. They hadn't been able to go earlier, because it had been too dangerous after the federal troops had occupied the village. They didn't know when they left that the baby would arrive so soon, for just as they left Rosaura had gone into labor.

Tita had no choice but to go to her sister's bedside, hoping it wouldn't be for long.

She didn't have the least interest in seeing the little boy, girl, whatever.

She hadn't anticipated Pedro getting captured by the federales and summarily detained from getting the doctor, or Mama Elena and Chencha being unable to return because of shooting breaking out in the village that forced them to take refuge with the Lobos; so it turned out she was the only one present at the birth of her nephew. She! She alone!

In the hours she spent by her sister's side she learned more than in all the years she'd studied in the village school. She denounced all her teachers and her mama for never having told her how to deliver a baby. What good did it do her now to know the names of the planets and Carreno's manual from A to Z if her sister was practically dead and she couldn't help her. Rosaura had gained sixty-five pounds during her pregnancy, which made the labor to deliver her first child even more difficult. Even allowing for her sister's excessive bulk, Tita noticed that Rosaura's body was extraordinarily swollen. First her feet swelled up, then her face and hands. Tita wiped the sweat from her brow and tried to revive her but Rosaura didn't even seem to hear her.

Tita had seen some animals being born, but those experiences didn't help with this birth. She had been only a spectator on those occasions. The animals knew everything they had to do, whereas she knew nothing. She had prepared sheets, hot water, and sterilized scissors. She knew she had to cut the umbilical cord, but she didn't know how, or when, nor to what length. She knew there was a series of little things she had to do for the baby as soon as it entered this world, but she didn't know what they were. The only thing she knew was that first it had to be born, any moment now! Tita peeked between her sister's legs repeatedly, but nothing. Nothing but a tunnel, dark, silent, deep. Kneeling and facing Rosaura, Tita made an urgent request to Nacha to enlighten her at this time.

If Nacha could tell her recipes in the kitchen, she should also be able to help in this emergency. Somebody up there had better attend to Rosaura, because there was nobody down here to do so.

She didn't know how long she knelt in prayer, but when she pried her eyes open, the dark tunnel of a moment before had been transformed into a red river, an erupting volcano, a rending of paper. Her sister's flesh opened to make way for life. Tita would never forget that sound, or the way her nephew's head had emerged, triumphant in his struggle for life. It was not a beautiful head; indeed, it was shaped like a cone of brown sugar because of the pressure his bones had been under for so many hours. But to Tita it seemed the most beautiful head she'd ever seen.

The baby's cries filled all the empty space in Tita's heart. She realized that she was feeling a new love: for life, for this child, for Pedro, even for the sister she had despised for so long. She took the child in her hands, carried him to Rosaura, and they wept together for a while, holding the child. She knew exactly what to do for the baby afterward from the instructions Nacha whispered in her ear: cut the umbilical cord, in the right place at the right time, clean him with sweet almond oil, bind the navel, and finally dress him. No problem, she knew how to put on the undershirt, and the shirt, the swaddling band around his belly, the diaper, the flannel to cover his legs, the little jacket, the socks and shoes, and last of all a soft wrap to keep his hands crossed on his chest so he wouldn't scratch his face. When Mama Elena and Chencha finally arrived home that night with the Lobos, they all admired the professional job Tita had done. Wrapped up like a taco, the baby was sleeping peacefully.

Pedro made it back with Dr. Brown the next day, after the federales set him free. His return was a relief to all of them.

They had feared for his life. Now their only worry was Rosaura's health, since she was still swollen and was very weak. Dr. Brown examined her thoroughly. That was when they discovered how dangerous the birth had been. According to the doctor, Rosaura had suffered an attack of eclampsia that could have killed her. He was amazed that Tita had been able to assist at the birth so calmly and deliberately, and under such unfavorable conditions. Well, who knows what really excited his admiration, whether it was just the way Tita had delivered the baby by herself, with no experience, or how the toothy little girl he remembered had become a beautiful woman without his having noticed.

No woman had attracted him since the death of his wife five years before. The pain of losing her, practically as a newlywed, had made him impervious to love all these years. What a strange sensation he felt when he looked at Tita. A tingling sensation ran through his body, rousing and quickening his sleeping senses. He looked at her as if seeing her for the first time. How lovely her teeth seemed now, assuming their true proportion within the perfect harmony of delicate features that formed her face.

His thoughts were interrupted by Mama Elena's voice.

"Doctor, won't it be too much trouble for you to come here twice a day until my daughter is out of danger?"

"Certainly not! First, it's my duty, and second it's a pleasure to visit your lovely home."

It was fortunate indeed that Mama Elena was so worried about Rosaura's health that she didn't see the way John Brown's eyes lit up with admiration when he looked at Tita, because if she had, she never would have opened the door of her home to him so confidently.

Right now the doctor didn't seem a problem to

Mama Elena; her only worry was that Rosaura didn't have any milk.

Fortunately they found a wet nurse in the village whom they hired to nurse the baby. One of Nacha's relatives, she had just had her eighth child and was grateful for the honor of feeding Mama Elena's grandson. For a month she performed marvelously; then one morning, while on her way to the village to visit her family, she was struck by a stray bullet from a battle between the rebels and the federales and was mortally wounded. One of her relatives arrived at the ranch to bring them the news, just as Tita and Chencha were combining all the ingredients for the mole in a large earthenware pan.

That is the final step, which is done when all the ingredients have been ground as indicated in the recipe. Combine them in a large pan, add the cut up turkey, the chocolate, and sugar to taste. As soon as the mixture thickens, remove it from the heat.

Tita finished preparing the mole alone, since the minute she heard the news, Chencha left for the village to try to find another nurse for Tita's nephew. She returned that evening without success. The baby was crying angrily. They tried giving him cow's milk, but he rejected it. Then Tita tried giving him tea, as Nacha had done for her, but it was no use: the child rejected that, too. It occurred to Tita that if she put on the rebozo that Lupita the wet nurse had left behind, its familiar smell might soothe the baby; it had just the opposite effect, and he cried even harder, because its smell told him he was going to be fed and he couldn't understand why there was this delay. He was frantically trying to find the milk in Tita's breasts. If there was one thing Tita couldn't resist, it was a hungry person asking for food. But she had none to give. It was sheer torture. When she couldn't stand it a moment longer, she pulled open her blouse and offered the baby her breast. She knew it was completely dry, but at least it would act as a pacifier and keep him occupied while she decided what to do to appease his hunger.

The baby clamped desperately onto the nipple and he sucked and he sucked. When she saw the boy's face slowly grow peaceful and when she heard the way he was swallowing, she began to suspect that something extraordinary had happened. Was it possible that she was feeding the baby? She removed the boy from her breast: a thin stream of milk sprayed out. Tita could not understand it. It wasn't possible for an unmarried woman to have milk, short of a supernatural act, unheard of in these times. When the child realized he'd been separated from his meal, he started to wail again. Immediately Tita let him take her breast, until his hunger was completely satisfied and he was sleeping peacefully, like a saint. She was so absorbed in her contemplation of the child that she didn't notice Pedro coming into the kitchen. At this moment, Tita looked like Ceres herself, goddess of plenty.

Pedro wasn't surprised in the least, nor did he need an explanation. Smiling delightedly he went over to them, bent down, and kissed Tita on the forehead. Tita took the child, now satisfied, from her breast. Then Pedro's eyes beheld a sight he had only glimpsed before through her clothing: Tita s breasts.

Tita tried to cover herself with her blouse. Pedro helped her in silence, with great tenderness. As he did, a succession of conflicting emotions took hold of them: love, desire, tenderness, lust, shame . . . fear of discovery. The sound of Mama Elena's footsteps on the wooden floor warned them of the danger in time. Tita finished adjusting her blouse properly and Pedro moved away from her as Mama Elena came into the kitchen. When she opened the kitchen door, she didn't see anything that wasn't socially acceptable—nothing to make her worry.

Still, there was something in the air, she could smell it, and she sharpened her senses to try to figure out what was troubling her.

"Tita, how is the child? Did you manage to get him to eat something?"

"Yes, Mami, he took some tea and fell asleep."

"Thank God! Then Pedro, why aren't you taking the child to his mother? Children shouldn't be away from their mothers."

Pedro left with the child in his arms, while Mama Elena carefully observed Tita, who had a sparkle in her eye that Mama Elena didn't like at all.

"Is the chocolate atole ready for your sister?"

"Yes, Mami."

"Give it to me so I can take it to her, she needs to drink it day and night so her milk will come in."

But as much chocolate atole as she drank, Rosaura never had any milk. Whereas Tita had enough milk to feed Roberto and two more babies besides, if she'd wanted to, from that day on. As Rosaura was still weak sometimes, no one was surprised that Tita took over her nephew's feeding; what no one found out was how she fed him, since Tita, with Pedro's help, was very careful not to let anyone see her.

For that reason, the baby, instead of driving them apart, actually brought them closer together. It was as if the child's mother was Tita, and not Rosaura. That's how she felt and acted. The day of the baptism, how proudly she carried her nephew, showing him off to all of the guests. Rosaura had to limit her appearance to the church, since she felt too sick. So Tita took her place at the banquet.

John Brown, the doctor, was watching Tita, charmed by her. He couldn't take his eyes off of her. John had attended the baptism just to see if he could speak to her alone. Even though he saw her every day during the housecalls he made to Rosaura, he had never had a chance to speak freely to her without someone else being there. When Tita walked by the table where he was sitting, he got up and went over to her on the pretext of admiring the baby.

"How nice the child looks with such a beautiful aunt holding him!"

"Thank you, Doctor."

"He isn't even your own son. Imagine how pretty you will look with one of your own."

A look of sorrow crossed Tita's face. John saw it and said:

"Forgive me, it seems I've said something wrong."

"No, it's not that. I can't marry or have children because I have to take care of my mother until she dies."

"But how can that be! It's absurd."

"But it's true. Now, please excuse me, I have to attend to my guests."

Tita quickly moved away from John, leaving him completely shaken. She was too, but she recovered when she felt Roberto in her arms. What did her fate matter, when she had this child near her, this child who was as much hers as anybody's? Really, she did a mother's work without the official title. Pedro and Roberto were hers and that was all she needed.

Tita was so happy that she didn't realize that her mother—like John, except that she had a different motive—was not letting her out of sight for a single instant. She was convinced that something was going on between Tita and Pedro. Trying to catch them, she didn't even eat, and she was so intent on the task of watching them that she hardly noticed the success of the party. Everyone agreed that a large part of the credit should go to Tita; the mole she had prepared was delicious! She kept getting compliments on her skill as a cook, and everyone wanted to know what her secret was. It was really a shame that as Tita was answering this question, saying that her secret was to prepare the mole with a lot of love, Pedro happened to be nearby, and that they looked at each other for a fraction of a second like conspirators, remembering when Tita had been bent over the grinding stone; for the eagle eye of Mama Elena saw the spark that flew between them from twenty feet away, and it troubled her deeply.

Actually, among all the guests, she was the only one who felt at all troubled. Everyone, oddly enough, was in a euphoric mood after eating the mole; it had made them unusually cheerful. They laughed and carried on as they never had before and wouldn't again for a long time. The threat of the revolution hung over them, bringing famine and death in its wake. But for those few moments they all seemed determined to forget the bullets flying in the village.

The only one who never lost her control was Mama Elena, who was too busy looking for a way to vent her bad temper. When Tita was standing near enough not to miss a single word, she remarked to Father Ignacio in a loud voice:

"The way things are going, Father, I worry that some day my daughter Rosaura will need a doctor and we won't be able to get one, like when Roberto was born. As soon as she gets her strength back, I think it would be best if she went to live with my cousin in San Antonio, with her husband and little boy. She would receive better medical attention there."

"I don't agree, doña Elena, because of the political situation. You need a man to defend the house."

"I've never needed a man for anything; all by myself, I've done all right with my ranch and my daughters. Men aren't that important in this life, Father"—she said emphatically—"nor is the revolution as dangerous as you make it out! It's worse to have chiles with no water around!"

"Well, that is true!" he replied laughing. "Ah, doña Elena, always so clever. And tell me, have you thought about where Pedro will work in San Antonio?"

"He can start as an accountant in my cousin's company; he wouldn't have any problem, his English is perfect."

Those words echoed like cannons inside Tita's head.

She couldn't let it happen. They couldn't take the child away from her now. She had to keep that from ever happening. Meanwhile, Mama Elena had managed to ruin the party for her. The first party in her life that she had enjoyed.

TO BE CONTINUED . . .

Next month's recipe:

Northern-style Chorizo

CHAPTER FIVE

MAY

Northern-style Chorizo

INGREDIENTS:

8 kilos pork loin
2 kilos pork head or scraps
1 kilo chiles anchos
60 grams cumin
60 grams oregano
30 grams pepper
6 grams cloves
2 cups garlic
2 liters apple vinegar
1/4 kilo salt

PREPARATION:

Heat the vinegar and add the chiles after removing the seeds. When the mixture comes to a boil, remove the pan from the heat and put a lid on it, so that the chiles soften.

Chencha set the cover on the pan and ran to the kitchen garden to help Tita look for worms. Mama Elena kept coming into the kitchen to supervise the preparation of the sausage and the preparations for her bath, and they were behind on both. Ever since Pedro, Rosaura, and Roberto had gone to live in San Antonio, Tita had lost all interest in life, except for her interest in feeding worms to a helpless pigeon. Apart from that, the house could fall down and it wouldn't have mattered to her.

Chencha didn't even want to think about what would happen if Mama Elena came in and found that Tita wasn't helping make the sausage.

They had decided to make the sausage because it's one of the best ways to use the meat from a pig economically and get food that both tastes good and keeps well, without risk of spoiling. They had also prepared a lot of salt pork, ham, bacon, and lard. They had to get every possible use from this pig, one of the few animals that had survived the visit the revolutionary army had made to the ranch a few days before.

When the rebels arrived, only Mama Elena, Tita, Chencha, and two farmhands, Rosalio and Guadalupe, were at the ranch. Nicholas, the manager, had not yet come back with the cattle he had been forced to go buy; the scarcity of food had made them kill the animals they depended on, which he was now trying to replace. He had taken along two of his most trustworthy workers to help him, leaving his son Felipe in charge of the ranch; but Mama Elena had relieved him of that duty, sending him to San Antonio, Texas, for news of Pedro and his family. They were afraid something bad had happened to them, since they hadn't heard a thing.

Rosalio rode up at a gallop to tell them that a troop of soldiers was approaching the ranch. Mama Elena immediately picked up her shotgun; as she cleaned it she plotted how to hide her valuables from the greed and gluttony of these men. No one had ever had anything good to say about these revolutionaries—and obviously what she had heard could scarcely be unreliable, since she'd gotten it from Father Ignacio and the mayor of Piedras Negras. They had told her how the rebels entered houses, destroyed everything, and raped all the women in their path. She ordered Tita, Chencha, and the pig to stay hidden in the cellar.

When the revolutionaries arrived, they were met by Mama Elena at the entrance of the house. She had her shotgun hidden in her petticoats, and she had Rosalio and Guadalupe at her side. Her gaze met that of the captain in charge, and he knew immediately from the steeliness of her eyes that they were in the presence of a woman to be reckoned with.

"Good afternoon, señora, are you the owner of this ranch?"

"Yes, I am. What is it you want?"

"We've come to ask you to volunteer to help the cause."

"I'll volunteer to tell you to take whatever you like from the corn crib and the stable. But that is the limit; I won't allow you to touch anything inside my house. Understand? Those things are for my cause."

The captain, laughing, snapped to attention and answered her:

"Understood, my general."

This joke tickled all the soldiers, and they laughed heartily, but the captain could see you didn't fool around with Mama Elena, what she said was serious, very serious.

Trying not to be intimidated by the fierce domineering look he got from her, he ordered the soldiers to inspect the ranch. They didn't find much, a little corn for scattering and eight chickens. A frustrated sergeant came back to the captain and said:

"The old lady must have everything hidden in the house. Let me go in and take a look around!"

Mama Elena put her finger on the trigger and answered:

"I'm not joking. I repeat: no one is setting foot in my house!"

Laughing, swinging the chickens he was carrying in his hands, the sergeant started toward the door. Mama Elena raised the gun, braced herself against the wall so she wouldn't be knocked to the ground by the kick of the gun, and shot the chickens. Bits of chicken flew in every direction along with the smell of burnt feathers.

Shaking, Rosalio and Guadalupe got out their pistols, fully convinced that this was their last day on earth. The soldier next to the captain was going to shoot Mama Elena, but the captain motioned him to stop. They were all waiting for his order to attack.

"I have a very good aim and a very bad temper, Captain. The next shot is for you, and I assure you that I can shoot you before they can kill me, so it would be best for us to respect each other. If we die, no one will miss me very much, but won't the nation mourn your loss?"

It really was hard to meet Mama Elena's gaze, even for the captain. There was something daunting about it. It produced a nameless fear in those who suffered it; they felt tried and convicted for their offenses. They fell prisoner to a childlike fear of maternal authority.

"You're right. Don't worry, no one is going to kill you, or fail to respect you, that's for sure! Such a valiant woman will always have my admiration." He turned to his soldiers and said:

"No one is to set foot in the house; see what else you can find here and let's go."

What they found was the huge dovecote formed by two slopes of the roof on the enormous house. To get to it you had to climb up a twenty-foot ladder. Three rebels

climbed up and stood there stunned for some time before they were able to move. They were impressed by
the dovecote's size and by the darkness and the cooing
of the doves gathered there, coming and going through
narrow side windows. They closed the door and the windows so none of them could get away and set about
trapping the pigeons and doves.

They rounded up enough to feed the entire batallion
for a week. Before the troops withdrew, the captain rode
around the back patio, inhaling deep whiffs of the scent
of roses that still clung indelibly to this place. He closed
his eyes and was still for quite a while. Returning to
Mama Elena's side, he asked her:

"I understood you had three daughters. Where are
they?"

"The oldest and youngest live in the United States,
the other died."

The news seemed to move the captain. In a barely
audible voice, he replied:

"That is a pity, a very great pity."

He took leave of Mama Elena with a bow. They left
peacefully, just as they had come, and Mama Elena was
quite disconcerted by the way they had treated her; it
didn't fit the picture of the heartless ruffians she'd been
expecting. From that day on she would not express any
opinion about the revolutionaries. What she never
learned was that this captain was the same Juan Alejandrez who had carried off her daughter Gertrudis some
months before.

They were even on that score, for the captain remained ignorant of the large number of chickens that
Mama Elena had hidden behind the house, buried in

ashes. They had managed to kill twenty before the troops arrived. The chickens are filled with ground wheat or oats and then placed, feathers and all, into a glazed earthenware pot. The pot is covered tightly using a narrow strip of cloth; that way the meat can be kept for more than a week.

It had been a common practice on the ranch since ancient times, when they had to preserve animals after a hunting party.

When she came out of hiding, Tita immediately missed the constant cooing of the doves, which had been part of her everyday life ever since she was born. This sudden silence made her feel her loneliness all the more. It was then that she really felt the loss of Pedro, Rosaura, and Roberto. She hurried up the rungs of the enormous ladder that went to the dovecote, but all she found there was the usual carpet of feathers and droppings.

The wind stole through the open door and lifted some feathers that fell on a carpet of silence. Then she heard a tiny sound: a little newborn pigeon had been spared from the massacre. Tita picked it up and got ready to go back down, but first she stopped for a moment to look at the cloud of dust the soldiers' horses left in their wake. She wondered why they hadn't done anything to hurt her mother. While she was in her hiding place, she had prayed that nothing bad would happen to Mama Elena, but unconsciously she had hoped that when she got out she would find her mother dead.

Ashamed of these thoughts, she placed the pigeon between her breasts to free her hands for the dangerous ladder, and climbed down from the dovecote. From then on, her main interest lay in feeding that pathetic baby pigeon. Only then did life seem to make a little sense. It didn't compare with the satisfaction derived from nursing a human being, but in some way it was similar.

The milk in her breasts had dried up overnight from the pain of her separation from her nephew. As she looked for worms, she kept wondering who was feeding Roberto and how he was eating. Those thoughts tortured her night and day. She hadn't been able to sleep, for a whole month. The only thing she accomplished during this period was to quintuple the size of her enormous bedspread. Chencha came to shake her out of her rueful thoughts; she gave her a few pushes to get her into the kitchen. She sat her down in front of the stone metate and set her to grinding the spices with the chiles. To make this process easier, it helps to add a few drops of vinegar from time to time as you're grinding. Last of all, mix the meat, finely chopped and ground, with the chiles and spices and let the mixture rest for a while, preferably overnight.

They had barely begun their grinding, when Mama Elena came into the kitchen, asking why the tub for her bath had not been filled. She didn't like to bathe too late, or her hair wouldn't dry properly.

Preparing Mama Elena's bath was quite a ceremony. The water had to be heated with lavender flowers, Mama Elena's favorite scent. Then this "decoction" had to be strained through a clean cloth and a few drops of aguardiente added to it. Finally, she had to carry buckets of hot water, one after another, to "the dark room"—a small room at one end of the house, next to the kitchen. As its name indicated, this room didn't receive any light, since it had no windows. All it had was a narrow door. Inside, in the middle of the room, there was a large tub into which the water was poured. Next to it, there was a pewter pitcher for the aloe water used in washing Mama Elena's hair.

Only Tita, whose mission it was to serve her until death, was allowed to be present during this ritual, to see her mother naked. No one else. That's why the room had been built to prevent anyone seeing in. Tita first had to wash her mother's body and then her hair, and then finally she had to go iron the clothes that Mama Elena would put on when she got out of the tub, while Mama Elena stayed in the tub relaxing and enjoying the water.

At a summons from her mother, Tita helped her to dry herself and put on her warm clothes as quickly as possible, so she wouldn't catch cold. Afterward, Tita opened the door just an inch, so the room would cool down a little bit and Mama Elena's body wouldn't suffer from an abrupt change of temperature. The whole while, Tita brushed her hair in that room lit only by the weak beam of light through the crack at the door, which created an eerie atmosphere as it revealed strange shapes in the rising steam. She brushed Mama Elena's hair until it was thoroughly dry, braided it, and that completed the liturgy. Tita always thanked God that her mother only bathed once a week, because otherwise her life would be a real cross to bear.

In Mama Elena's opinion, both her bath and her meals were the same story: no matter how hard Tita tried she always got an infinite number of things wrong. Either her blouse had a wrinkle, or there wasn't enough hot water, or her braid came out uneven—in short, it seemed

Mama Elena's genius was for finding fault. But she had never found as many faults as today. And that was because Tita really had been careless with all the fine points of the ceremony. The water was so hot that Mama Elena burned her feet when she got in, Tita had forgotten the aloe water for her hair, burned the bottom of Mama Elena's chemise, opened the door too far, and finally, got Mama Elena's attention the hard way and was scolded and sent from the bathroom.

Tita was striding toward the kitchen, the dirty clothes under her arm, bemoaning the rebuke she'd received and her boundless failings. What grieved her the most was the extra work burning the clothes meant. It was the second time in her life that this sort of disaster had occurred. Now she had to wet the reddish stains with a solution of potassium chlorate, plain water, and soft alkaline lye, scrubbing them repeatedly until she managed to get them out, and this difficult job was added to her job of washing the black clothes her mother wore. To wash those, she had to dissolve cow bile in a small amount of boiling water, fill a soft sponge with it, and use it to dampen the clothes all over; then she had to rinse the clothes in clear water and hang them out to dry.

Tita rubbed and rubbed the clothes as many times as she had rubbed Roberto's diapers to remove the stains. What worked was to heat up a little urine, dip the stain in it for a minute, and wash it afterward in water. That is the one way to make stains fade away. But no matter how much she soaked the diaper in urine, she couldn't get rid of the horrid black color. Then she realized it wasn't Roberto's diaper she was holding, but her mother's clothes. They had been soaking in the pot where she had left them since morning, forgetting to wash them in the sink. Embarrassed, she set about correcting her error.

Settled in the kitchen, Tita resolved to pay more attention to what she was doing. She had to suppress the memories that tormented her or Mama Elena's fury would erupt any moment.

Since she had left the sausage resting when she had gone to prepare Mama Elena's bath, enough time had passed to go on to stuffing the casings.

The casings should be pork intestines, cleaned and cured. The sausages are filled using a funnel. Tie them off tightly, four fingers apart, and poke them with a needle so the air can escape, because air can spoil the sausage. It's very important to squeeze the sausage firmly while filling it, so you don't leave any spaces.

Hard as Tita tried to stem the memories that assaulted her and caused her to make more mistakes, holding a large sausage in her hands she couldn't keep from remembering the summer night when they all slept outside on the patio. During the dog days, they hung giant hammocks on the patio, because of the unbearable heat. They set a large earthenware jar full of ice on a table and inside they placed a cut-up watermelon in case someone was hot and got up in the middle of the night wanting to eat a slice to cool down. Mama Elena was a specialist in cutting the watermelon: taking a sharp knife, she would drive the point in so it penetrated just to the end of the green part of the rind, without touching the heart of the watermelon.

She made her cuts through the rind with such mathematical precision that when she was done, she could pick up the watermelon and give it a single blow against a stone, in a particular spot, and like magic the watermelon rind would open like the petals of a flower, leaving the heart intact on the table. Unquestionably, when it came to dividing, dismantling, dismembering, desolating, detaching, dispossessing, destroying, or dominating, Mama Elena was a pro. After she died, no one ever came close to accomplishing the same feats, with the watermelon.

From her hammock Tita heard someone get up for a chunk of watermelon. This awakened in her the urge to go to the bathroom. She had been drinking beer all day long, not to cool off, but to make more milk to nurse her nephew.

He was sleeping peacefully next to her sister. Getting up in the dark, she couldn't see a thing—there wasn't a glimmer of light. She was walking toward the bathroom, trying to remember where the hammocks were; she didn't want to stumble into anybody.

Pedro, sitting in his hammock, was eating a slice of watermelon and thinking of Tita. Having her so near made him feel a tremendous excitement. He couldn't sleep thinking of her there a few steps from him . . . and from Mama Elena, too, of course. He heard the sound of footsteps in the shadows and stopped breathing for a few moments. It had to be Tita, her distinctive fragrance wafted toward him on the breeze, a mixture of jasmine and cooking odors that was hers alone. For a moment he thought that Tita had gotten up to look for him. The sound of her approaching footsteps blended with the violent beating of his heart. But no, the steps were moving away from him, to the bathroom. Pedro got up as quiet as a cat and followed her.

Tita was surprised to feel someone pull her toward him and cover her mouth, but she realized who it was immediately and didn't offer any resistance as the hand first slid down her neck to her breasts and then explored her entire body.

While she was receiving a kiss on the lips, Pedro took her hand in his and invited her to explore his body. Tita timidly touched the hard muscles on Pedro's arms and chest; lower down, she felt a red-hot coal that throbbed through his clothes. She removed her hand, frightened not by her discovery but by a cry from Mama Elena.

"Tita, where are you?"

"Right here, Mami, I'm going to the bathroom."

Fearful that her mother would suspect something, Tita hurried back to bed where she passed a tortured night, enduring her desire to urinate along with another urge. Her sacrifice didn't do a bit of good: the following day, Mama Elena—who for a while seemed to have changed her mind about sending Pedro and Rosaura to Texas—speeded up her plans for their departure; three days later they had left the ranch.

Those memories were banished by Mama Elena's entry into the kitchen. Tita let the sausage she was holding fall to the floor. She suspected that her mother was able to read her thoughts. Behind Mama Elena came Chencha, weeping unconsolably.

"Don't cry, child. It annoys me to see you cry. What has happened?"

"Felipe has come back and he says he's dead!"

"Who says? Who's dead?"

"Well, the child!"

"What child?" Tita demanded.

"Well, what child do you think! Well, your nephew; whatever he ate, it didn't agree with him and so, he died!"

Tita felt the household crashing down around her head. The blow, the sound of all the dishes breaking into a thousand pieces. She sprang to her feet.

"Sit down and get back to work. I don't want any tears. Poor child, I hope the Good Lord has taken him in all his glory, but we can't give in to sorrow; there's work to do. First work, then do as you please, except crying, do you hear?"

Tita felt a violent agitation take possession of her being: still fingering the sausage, she calmly met her mother's gaze and then, instead of obeying her order, she started to tear apart all the sausages she could reach, screaming wildly.

"Here's what I do with your orders! I'm sick of them! I'm sick of obeying you!"

Mama Elena went to her, picked up a wooden spoon, and smashed her across the face with it.

"You did it, you killed Roberto!" screamed Tita, beside herself, and she ran from the room, wiping the blood that dripped from her nose. She took the pigeon and a pail full of worms and climbed up to the dovecote.

Mama Elena ordered them to remove the ladder and let her stay up there overnight. Mama Elena and Chencha finished filling the sausages in silence. Mama Elena was always such a perfectionist and so careful to get all the air out of the sausage, no one could explain it when they discovered a week later that all the sausages in the cellar were swarming with worms.

The next morning she ordered Chencha to get Tita down from the dovecote. Mama Elena couldn't do it because her one fear in life was heights. She couldn't bear the thought of having to climb up that ladder, twenty feet high, to get to the little door that would have to be opened in order to get in. She feigned a convenient pride, more than she actually had, and ordered someone else to bring Tita down, even though she felt a strong urge to go up there and personally drag Tita down by the hair.

Chencha found Tita holding the pigeon. She didn't seem to realize it was dead. She was trying to feed it some more worms. The poor thing probably died of indigestion because Tita fed it too much. Tita looked up, her eyes vacant, and stared at Chencha as if she had never seen her before.

Chencha came down saying Tita was acting like a crazy person and refused to leave the dovecote.

"Fine, if she is acting crazy, then I'm going to put her in an asylum. There's no place in this house for maniacs!"

And without a moment's delay she sent Felipe for Dr. Brown to take Tita to an insane asylum. The doctor arrived, listened to Mama Elena's version of the story, and set off up the ladder to the dovecote.

He found Tita naked, her nose broken, her whole body covered with pigeon droppings. A few feathers were clinging to her skin and hair. As soon as she saw the doctor, she ran to the corner and curled up in a fetal position.

No one knew how much she told Dr. Brown during the hours he spent there, but toward dark he brought

Tita down, now dressed, and she got into his carriage and drove off with him.

Chencha, weeping, was running alongside the carriage as they left and barely managed to toss onto Tita's shoulders the enormous bedspread she had knit during her endless nights of insomnia. It was so large and heavy it didn't fit inside the carriage. Tita grabbed it so tightly that there was no choice but to let it drag behind the carriage like the huge train of a wedding gown that stretched for a full kilometer. Tita used any yarn she happened to have in her bedspread, no matter what the color, and it revealed a kaleidoscopic combination of colors, textures, and forms that appeared and disappeared as if by magic in the gigantic cloud of dust that rose up behind it.

TO BE CONTINUED . . .

Next month's recipe:

A Recipe for Making Matches

CHAPTER SIX

JUNE

*A Recipe
for Making Matches*

INGREDIENTS:

1 ounce powdered potassium
  nitrate
1/2 ounce minium
1/2 ounce powdered gum arabic
1 dram phosphorus
saffron
cardboard

PREPARATION:

The gum arabic is dissolved in enough hot water to form a paste that is not too thick; when the paste is ready, the phosphorus is added and dissolved into it, and the same is done with the potassium nitrate. Then enough minium is added to color the mixture.

Tita was watching in silence as Dr. Brown completed these procedures.

She was sitting by the window of the doctor's little laboratory in back of the patio behind his house. The light that filtered in through the window struck her shoulders and provided a faint sensation of warmth, so slight it was almost imperceptible. A chronic chill kept her from feeling warm, in spite of being covered with her heavy woolen bedspread. One of her greatest interests was still working on the bedspread each night, with yarn John had bought for her.

Of the whole house, this was the place they both

liked best. Tita had discovered it the week she arrived at
Dr. Brown's. John, ignoring Mama Elena's order, had not
put Tita in a madhouse but had taken her to live with
him. Tita would never be able to thank him enough. In a
madhouse she might have become truly insane. But here,
with John's warmth toward her in word and manner, she
felt better each day. Her arrival there was like a dream.
Among the blurry images, she remembered the terrible
pain she felt when the doctor had set her broken nose.

Afterward, John's large, loving hands, had taken off
her clothes and bathed her and carefully removed the
pigeon droppings from her body, leaving her clean and
sweet-smelling. Finally, he gently brushed her hair and
put her in a bed with starched sheets.

Those hands had rescued her from horror and she
would never forget it.

Some day, when she felt like talking, she would tell
John that; but now, she preferred silence. There were
many things she needed to work out in her mind, and
she could not find the words to express the feelings
seething inside her since she left the ranch. She was
badly shaken. The first few days she didn't even want to
leave her room; her food was brought to her there by
Katy, a seventy-year-old North American woman, who
besides being in charge of the kitchen also took care of
Alex, the doctor's little boy, whose mother had died
when he was born. Tita heard Alex laughing and running
in the patio, but she felt no desire to meet him.

Sometimes Tita didn't even taste her food, which was
bland and didn't appeal to her. Instead of eating, she
would stare at her hands for hours on end. She would
regard them like a baby, marveling that they belonged to

her. She could move them however she pleased, yet she didn't know what to do with them, other than knitting. She had never taken time to stop and think about these things. At her mother's, what she had to do with her hands was strictly determined, no questions asked. She had to get up, get dressed, get the fire going in the stove, fix breakfast, feed the animals, wash the dishes, make the beds, fix lunch, wash the dishes, iron the clothes, fix dinner, wash the dishes, day after day, year after year. Without pausing for a moment, without wondering if this was what she wanted. Now, seeing her hands no longer at her mother's command, she didn't know what to ask them to do, she had never decided for herself before. They could do anything or become anything. They could turn into birds and fly into the air! She would like them to carry her far away, as far as possible. Going to the window facing the patio, she raised her hands to heaven; she wanted to escape from herself, didn't want to think about making a choice, didn't want to talk again. She didn't want her words to shriek her pain.

She yearned with all her soul to be borne off by her hands. She stood that way for a while, looking at the deep blue of the sky around her motionless hands. Tita thought the miracle was actually occurring when she saw her fingers turning into a thin cloud rising to the sky. She prepared to ascend drawn by a superior power, but nothing happened. Disappointed, she discovered that the smoke wasn't hers.

It originated in a small room at the far end of the patio. Its chimney was emitting such a pleasant and familiar aroma that she opened the window to inhale it more deeply. Eyes closed, she saw herself beside Nacha on the kitchen floor making corn tortillas; she saw the pan where the most delicious casserole was cooking, and next to it, the beans just coming to a boil . . . not even hesitating, she decided to go see who was cooking. It couldn't be Katy. The person who produced this kind of smell really knew how to cook. Never having laid eyes on her, Tita felt she knew this person, whoever she was.

She strode across the patio and opened the door; there she met a pleasant woman around eighty years old. She looked a lot like Nacha. A thick braid was wound around her head, and she was wiping the sweat from her brow with her apron. Her features were plainly Indian. She was making tea in an earthenware pan.

She looked up and smiled kindly, inviting Tita to sit down next to her. Tita did so. The woman immediately offered her a cup of the delicious tea.

Tita sipped it slowly, drawing maximum pleasure from the aroma of the herbs, familiar and mysterious. How welcome its warmth and flavor!

She stayed with the woman for a little while. The woman didn't speak either, but it wasn't necessary. From the first, they had established a communication that went far beyond words.

From then on, Tita had visited her there every day. But gradually, Dr. Brown began to appear instead of the woman. The first time this happened it had surprised her —she wasn't expecting to see him there, nor the changes he had made in the room's furnishings.

Now the room contained many pieces of scientific equipment, test tubes, lamps, thermometers, and so on. . . . The little stove no longer occupied a central place;

it had been relegated to a tiny spot in the corner of the room. Moving it was not right, she felt, but since she did not want her lips to emit a single sound, she saved that opinion for later as well as her question about the whereabouts and identity of the woman. Besides, she had to admit that she also enjoyed John's company a good deal. There was just one difference: he did speak to her as he worked; but instead of cooking, he was testing theories scientifically.

He had inherited his fondness for experimentation from his grandmother, a Kikapu Indian who John's grandfather had captured and brought back to live with him, far from her tribe. Despite this and the fact that he married her, she was never accepted as his legal wife by the grandfather's proud, intensely Yankee family. So John's grandfather had built this room for her at the back of the house, where she could spend most of the day doing what interested her most: studying the curative properties of plants.

The room also served as her refuge from the family's attacks. One of their first was to give her the nickname "the Kikapu," instead of calling her by her real name, thinking that this would really upset her. For the Browns, the word Kikapu summed up everything that was most disagreeable in the world, but this was not at all the case with Morning Light. To her it meant just the opposite and was an enormous source of pride.

That is but one small example of the huge difference in ideas and opinions that existed between the representatives of these two very different cultures, a gulf that made it impossible for the Browns to feel any desire to learn about the customs and traditions of Morning Light.

Years passed before they began to discover a bit of the culture of "the Kikapu," when John's great-grandfather, Peter, was very sick with a lung disease. His face was constantly purple from his fits of coughing. He wasn't getting enough air. His wife Mary knew something about medicine, since her father was a doctor; she knew that in cases like his, the body of the sick person is producing too many red blood cells, so it is advisable to perform a bleeding to counter this imbalance and prevent this excess of blood cells from causing an infarction or a thrombosis, either of which can sometimes cause the death of the patient.

So John's great-grandmother, Mary, started preparing some leeches for bleeding her husband. As she worked, she felt quite proud of herself for being up-to-date with the best scientific knowledge, which allowed her to protect her family's health using an appropriate modern method—not like "the Kikapu" and her herbs!

The leeches are placed inside a glass containing a half a finger of water and left there for an hour. The part of the body to which they will be applied is washed with lukewarm sugar water. Meanwhile, the leeches are placed in a clean handkerchief, which is folded over them. Then they are turned out onto the part of the body where they are to be attached, held down firmly with the handkerchief, and pressed into the skin so they don't pierce some other spot. To continue the bloodletting after the leeches have been removed, it helps to rub the skin with warm water. To control the bleeding and close the wounds, cover them with cloth or poplar bark and then apply a poultice of bread crumbs and milk, which is removed when the wounds have formed scabs.

Mary followed all this to the letter, but when she pulled the leeches from Peter's arm he started to lose blood and the hemorrhage couldn't be stopped. When "the Kikapu" heard the desperate screams coming from the house, she ran to see what was happening. As soon as she went to the sick man and placed one of her hands on his wounds, the bleeding stopped. His family was absolutely astounded. Then she asked if they would please leave her alone with the sick man. After what they had just seen, no one dared to say no. She spent the entire afternoon at her father-in-law's bedside, singing strange melodies and applying curing herbs, wreathed in the smoke of the copal and incense she burned. It was well into night before the bedroom door opened and she came out, a cloud of incense surrounding her; behind her appeared Peter, completely restored.

After that, "the Kikapu" was their family doctor; within the North American community she was widely accepted as a miracle healer. John's grandfather wanted to build a much larger room for her to carry on her investigations, but she didn't want one. In the whole house she couldn't have a better place than her little laboratory. In her laboratory, John had passed most of his childhood and adolescence. He stopped visiting it when he entered the university, because the modern medical theories he was learning there were in strong opposition to his grandmother's theories, to everything he had learned from her. As medical research progressed, John remembered his grandmother's teachings and the initiation she had given him in medicine. Now, after years of work and study, he had returned to her laboratory. He was convinced that only there would he find the most advanced medicine—if he could scientifically prove all the miracle cures Morning Light had accomplished.

Tita loved to watch him work. With him there were always things to learn and discover, like now, when he was making matches and conducting a class on phosphorus and its properties at the same time.

"Phosphorus was discovered in 1669, by Brandt, a Hamburg chemist who was looking for the philosophers' stone. He believed that metal could be transmuted into gold by mixing it with extract of urine. Using this method, he obtained a luminous substance that burned with an intensity such as had never been seen before. For a long time phosphorus was obtained by vigorously heating the residue from evaporating urine in an earth retort the neck of which was submerged in water. Today it is extracted from the bones of animals, which contain phosphoric acid and lime."

Talking didn't make the doctor careless in his preparation of the matches. He had no trouble separating mental and physical activities. He could philosophize about even the most profound aspects of life without his hands pausing or making a mistake. While he was talking to Tita, he kept on making matches.

"Now that we have the phosphorus mixture, the next step is to prepare the cardboard for the matches. Dissolve a pound of potassium nitrate in a pound of water, stir in a little saffron to add color, and dip the cardboard in this solution. When it dries, cut the cardboard into narrow strips and place a little of the phosphorus mixture on the end of each strip. Allow the matches to dry, buried in sand."

While the strips were drying, the doctor showed Tita an experiment.

"While phosphorus doesn't combine with oxygen to burn at ordinary temperatures, it does burst into flame very rapidly at an elevated temperature; watch . . ."

The doctor placed a small amount of phosphorus in a tube that was closed at one end and full of mercury. He melted the phosphorus by holding the tube over the flame of a candle. Then, using a small bell jar containing oxygen, he transferred the gas to the jar very, very slowly. When the oxygen reached the top of the jar, where it encountered the melted phosphorus, an explosion occurred, brilliant, instantaneous, like a flash of lightning.

"As you see, within our bodies each of us has the elements needed to produce phosphorus. And let me tell you something I've never told a soul. My grandmother had a very interesting theory; she said that each of us is born with a box of matches inside us but we can't strike them all by ourselves; just as in the experiment, we need oxygen and a candle to help. In this case, the oxygen, for example, would come from the breath of the person you love; the candle could be any kind of food, music, caress, word, or sound that engenders the explosion that lights one of the matches. For a moment we are dazzled by an intense emotion. A pleasant warmth grows within us, fading slowly as time goes by, until a new explosion comes along to revive it. Each person has to discover what will set off those explosions in order to live, since the combustion that occurs when one of them is ignited is what nourishes the soul. That fire, in short, is its food. If one doesn't find out in time what will set off these explosions, the box of matches dampens, and not a single match will ever be lighted.

"If that happens, the soul flees from the body and goes to wander among the deepest shades, trying in vain to find food to nourish itself, unaware that only the body it left behind, cold and defenseless, is capable of providing that food."

How true these words were! Nobody knew it better than she.

Unfortunately, she had to admit that her own matches were damp and moldy. No one would ever be able to light another one again.

And the saddest thing was that she knew what set off her explosions, but each time she had managed to light a match, it had persistently been blown out.

As if reading her thoughts, John went on:

"That's why it's important to keep your distance from people who have frigid breath. Just their presence can put out the most intense fire, with results we're familiar with. If we stay a good distance away from those people, it's easier to protect ourselves from being extinguished." Taking one of Tita's hands in his, he added simply, "There are many ways to dry out a box of damp matches, but you can be sure, there is a cure."

Tita felt tears run down her face. Gently, John dried them with his handkerchief.

"You must of course take care to light the matches one at a time. If a powerful emotion should ignite them all at once they would produce a splendor so dazzling that it would illuminate far beyond what we can normally see; and then a brilliant tunnel would appear before our eyes, revealing the path we forgot the moment we were born, and summoning us to regain the divine origin we had lost. The soul ever longs to return to the place from which it came, leaving the body lifeless. . . . Ever since my grandmother died, I have been trying to demonstrate this theory scientifically. Perhaps someday I will succeed. What do you think?"

Dr. Brown remained silent to give Tita time to say something if she wished. But she was as silent as a stone.

"Well, I mustn't bore you with my talk. Let's take a break, but before we go, I'd like to show you a game my grandmother and I used to play. We spent most of the day here, and she taught me her secrets through games.

"She was a quiet woman, just like you. Sitting in front of her stove, her heavy braid wrapped around her head, she was always able to read my thoughts. I wanted to learn how to do it, so after much begging, she gave me my first lesson. She would write a sentence on the wall, using some invisible substance, without my seeing. When I looked at the wall at night, I would find out what she had written. Do you want to try it?"

From what he'd said, Tita realized that the woman she'd sat with so often was John's dead grandmother. Now she didn't need to ask him.

The doctor took a piece of phosphorus in a rag and gave it to Tita.

"I don't want to break the rule of silence you have imposed, so as a secret between us, I'm going to ask you to write the reason you won't talk on that wall over there as soon as I leave, all right? Tomorrow, I will divine the words before your eyes."

What the doctor neglected to tell Tita, of course, was that one of the properties of phosphorus was that it would glow in the dark, revealing what she had written on the wall. He had no real need of this subterfuge to know what she was thinking, but he thought it would be a good way for Tita to start communicating with the world again, if only in writing. John could see she was ready. When the doctor left, Tita took the phosphorus and went up to the wall.

That night, when John Brown entered the laboratory, he was pleased to see the writing on the wall, in firm phosphorescent letters: "Because I don't want to." With those words Tita had taken her first step toward freedom.

Meanwhile, she was staring up at the ceiling, unable to stop thinking of John's words: was it possible for her soul to stir again? With her whole being she wanted to believe that it was.

She had to find someone who could kindle her desire.

Could that someone be John? She was remembering the pleasant sensation that ran through her body when he took her hand in the laboratory. No. She wasn't sure. The only thing she was absolutely sure about was that she did not want to return to the ranch. She never wanted to live near Mama Elena again.

TO BE CONTINUED . . .

Next month's recipe:

Ox-Tail Soup

CHAPTER SEVEN

J ULY

Ox-Tail Soup

INGREDIENTS:

2 ox tails
1 onion
2 cloves garlic
4 tomatoes
1/4 kilo string beans
2 potatoes
4 chiles moritas

PREPARATION:

The cut-up ox tails are placed in a pan to cook with a chunk of onion, a clove of garlic, and salt and pepper to taste. It is advisable to add a little more water than you normally would, since you are making a soup. A good soup that's worth something has to be soupy without getting watery.

Soups can cure any illness, whether physical or mental—at least, that was Chencha's firm belief, and Tita's too, although she hadn't given sufficient credit to it for quite some time. But now it would have to be accepted as the truth.

About three months ago, after tasting a spoonful of soup that Chencha had made and brought to Dr. John Brown's house, Tita had returned to her senses.

She was at her high post in the window, looking through the glass at Alex, John's son, who was chasing doves on the patio.

She heard John's footsteps coming up the stairs. She was eagerly awaiting his customary visit. John's words were her only link with the world. If only she could talk, tell him how much his presence and his conversation meant to her. If only she could go down to Alex and kiss him like the son she didn't have, play with him until they were tired, if only she could remember how to cook so much as a couple of eggs, enjoy any kind of food, if only she could . . . return to life. She noticed a smell that struck her. A smell that was foreign to this house. John opened the door and stood there with a tray in his hands and a bowlful of ox-tail soup!

Ox-tail soup! She couldn't believe it. And behind John, in came Chencha, covered in tears. The embrace they exchanged was brief, because they didn't want the soup to get cold. With the first sip, Nacha appeared there at her side, stroking her hair as she ate, as she had done when she was little and was sick, kissing her forehead over and over. There were all the times with Nacha, the childhood games in the kitchen, the trips to the market, the still-warm tortillas, the colored apricot pits, the Christmas rolls, the smells of boiled milk, bread with cream, chocolate atole, cumin, garlic, onion. As always, throughout her life, with a whiff of onion, the tears began. She cried as she hadn't cried since the day she was born. How good it was to have a long talk with Nacha. Just like old times, when Nacha was still alive and they had so often made ox-tail soup together. Chencha and Tita laughed reliving those moments, and they cried remembering the steps of the recipe. At last Tita had been able to remember a recipe, once she had remembered the first step, chopping the onion.

The onion and the garlic are chopped very fine and placed in a little oil to fry; as soon as they become transparent, the potatoes, beans, and chopped tomatoes are stirred in until the flavors meld.

John interrupted these memories by bursting into the room, alarmed by the stream that was running down the stairs.

When he realized it was just Tita's tears, John blessed Chencha and her ox-tail soup for having accomplished what none of his medicines had been able to do—making Tita weep. Sorry to have interrupted, he started to leave the room. Tita's voice stopped him. That melodious voice had not spoken a word for six months.

"John! Please don't leave!"

At Tita's side, John watched her go from tears to smiles as she heard all the news and gossip from Chencha. The doctor learned that Mama Elena had forbidden visits to Tita. In the De la Garza family some things could be excused, but not disobedience, not questioning parental authority. Mama Elena would never forgive Tita, crazy or not, for blaming her for the death of Roberto. She had forbidden anyone to even mention Tita's name, just as she'd done with Gertrudis. Of course, Nicholas had returned recently with news of Gertrudis.

He had actually found her working in a brothel. He had delivered her clothes to her and she had given him a letter for Tita. Chencha gave it to her, and Tita read it to herself:

Dear Tita:

You can't know how grateful I am that you sent me my clothes. Fortunately, I was still here to get them. Tomorrow I will be leaving this place, which is not where I belong. I still don't know where that is, but I know that I have to find the right place for myself somewhere. I ended up here because I felt an intense fire inside; the man who picked me up in the field in effect saved my life. I hope to meet him again someday. He left because I had exhausted his strength, though he hadn't managed to quench the fire inside me. Now at last, after so many men have been with me, I feel a great relief. Perhaps someday I will return home and explain it to you.

I love you, your sister Gertrudis.

Tita put the letter in the pocket of her dress without a word. The fact that Chencha didn't ask her anything about the contents of the letter was a clear sign that she had already read it from one end to the other.

Later, the three of them, Tita, Chencha, and John, dried the bedroom, the stairs, and the bottom floor.

As they were saying good-bye, Tita told Chencha her decision never to go back to the ranch again; she asked her to tell Mama Elena. Chencha crossed the bridge between Eagle Pass and Piedras Negras for the hundredth time, without even realizing it, as she tried to think of the best way to break the news to Mama Elena. The watchmen for both countries let her do it, because they'd known her since she was a child. Besides, it was amusing to watch her go from one side to the other talking to herself and chewing on her rebozo. She felt as if her talent for invention had been paralyzed by terror.

Whatever version she gave, it was sure to infuriate Mama Elena. She had to invent one in which she, at least, got off scot free. To manage that she had to come up with an excuse that justified her visit with Tita. Mama Elena wouldn't swallow just anything. As if she didn't know it! She envied Tita for having had the courage to refuse to go back to the ranch. She wished she could do the same, but she didn't dare. She'd heard talk since she was a child about the bad things that happen to women who disobey their parents and masters and leave the house. They end up in the filthy gutter of a fast life. Nervous, she twisted her rebozo around and around, trying to squeeze out the best of her lies for this situation. It never failed. When the rebozo was turned a hundred times, a tale that fit the occasion always came to her. For her, lying was a survival skill that she had picked up as soon as she had arrived at the ranch. It was better to say that Father Ignacio had sent her to collect alms than to confess she had spilled the milk by chatting in the market. The judgment earned by the two stories was completely different.

Anything could be true or false, depending on whether one believed it. For example, nothing she had imagined about Tita's fate had proved to be true.

All these months she had been tormented thinking of the horrible things happening to Tita away from her kitchen. Surrounded by lunatics screaming obscenities, confined in a straitjacket, eating God knows what awful food away from home. She imagined that the food in a lunatic asylum, a gringo one to boot, must be the most disgusting in the world. Whereas in fact she'd found Tita looking pretty good, she'd never set foot in a nuthouse, she'd clearly been treated well in the doctor's house, and she hadn't been fed too poorly, since she looked to have put on a few pounds there. Still, no matter how much she had eaten, no one had given her anything like the beef-tail soup. That's one thing you can be sure of, or else why would she have cried so hard when she ate it?

Poor thing, surely now that she had left, Tita would resume weeping, tortured by memories, the thought that she would never again cook alongside Chencha. Yes, surely she was suffering deeply. Chencha could never have pictured Tita as she was then, radiant in a shiny moiré-inlaid satin dress, dining by moonlight and listening to a declaration of love. That would have been too much even for Chencha's feverish imagination. Tita was sitting by a fire roasting a marshmallow. Beside her John Brown was proposing marriage. Tita had agreed to accompany John under a half moon to a neighbor's ranch to celebrate the neighbor's discharge from military service. John had given her a beautiful dress he had bought for her in San Antonio, Texas, some time ago. Its multicolored fabric reminded her of the doves' plumage, the feathers around their necks, but without any sad associations with the distant day when she had shut herself in the dovecote. In fact, she felt completely recovered, ready to start a new life at John's side. They sealed their engagement with a gentle kiss on the lips. Tita didn't feel the same as when Pedro had kissed her, but she hoped that her spirit, which had been dampened for so long, would eventually be kindled by the presence of this wonderful man.

Finally, after walking for three hours, Chencha had the answer! As always, she had come up with the right lie. She would tell Mama Elena that she'd been passing through Eagle Pass and had seen a beggar on the street-corner, dressed in filthy, tattered clothes. Moved by pity, she had gone over to give her a coin and had been shocked at the discovery that the beggar was Tita. She had escaped from the lunatic asylum and was roaming the world to pay for the crime of having insulted her mother. Chencha had invited her to come back home, but Tita had refused. She didn't feel she deserved to return and live with such a good mother, and she had asked Chencha to please tell her mother that she loved her dearly and would never forget how much she had always done for her, and she promised that as soon as she became an honest woman she would return to be with her mother and give her all the love and respect that Mama Elena deserved.

Chencha figured this lie would cover her with glory, but unfortunately she wasn't able to tell it. That night, when she got to the house, a group of bandits attacked the ranch. They raped Chencha. Mama Elena, trying to defend her honor, suffered a strong blow to her spine and was left a paraplegic, paralyzed from the waist down. She was in no condition to hear this type of news, nor was Chencha in any condition to give it.

It was a good thing she hadn't said anything, because when Tita returned to the ranch after hearing about their calamity, Chencha's pious lie would have been shattered by Tita's splendid beauty and radiant energy. Her mother received her in silence. For the first time Tita firmly held her gaze, and Mama Elena lowered hers. There was a strange light in Tita's eyes.

Mama Elena had disowned her daughter. Without words, they made their mutual reproaches and thereby severed the strong tie of blood and obedience that had always bound them together, but could never be reestab-

lished. Tita knew perfectly well that her mother felt pro-
foundly humiliated because not only did she have to
allow Tita back into her house again but until she recovered she needed Tita to take care of her. For that reason,
Tita wanted with all her heart to give her the best possible care. She prepared her mother's meal very carefully
and especially the ox-tail soup, with the good intention
of serving it to her so that she would recover completely.

She poured the seasoned broth with the potatoes and
beans into the pan where she had placed the ox tails to
cook.

Once that is done, all that is necessary is to let the
ingredients simmer together for half an hour. Then, remove from the heat and serve piping hot.

Tita served the soup and took it up to her mother on
a beautiful silver tray covered by a napkin whose exquisite openwork cotton had been perfectly bleached and
starched.

Tita waited anxiously for her mother's reaction when
she had her first sip, but Mama Elena spit the soup on
the bedspread and yelled to Tita to get the tray out of
her sight immediately.

"But why?"

"Because it is nasty and bitter, and I don't want it.
Take it away! Don't you hear?"

Instead of obeying her, Tita turned away, trying not
to let her mother see her frustration. She didn't understand Mama Elena's attitude. She never had understood
it. It was beyond her comprehension that one person,
whatever her relationship with another, could reject a
kind gesture in such a brutal manner, just like that, so
high-handedly. She was sure the soup was delicious. She

had tasted it herself before bringing it up. It couldn't help but be good, she'd taken so much care in preparing it.

It made her feel like a fool for having returned to the ranch to care for her mother. It would have been better to stay at John's house without ever giving a thought to the fate that might befall Mama Elena. But the pangs of her conscience wouldn't let her. The only way Tita would ever be really free of her mother was when she died, and Mama Elena wasn't ready for that.

She felt an urge to run far, far away, to shield the tiny flame John had coaxed up inside her from her mother's chilling presence. It was as if Mama Elena's spit had landed dead-center on a fire that was about to catch and had put it out. Inside she felt the effects of snuffing the flame; smoke was rising into her throat, tightening into a thick knot and clouding her eyes and making her cry.

She opened the door quickly and ran out at the exact moment that John arrived to visit the patient. They crashed into each other. John held her in his arms just long enough to keep her from falling. His warm embrace saved Tita from freezing. They only touched for a few seconds but it was enough to rekindle her spirit. Tita was beginning to wonder if the feeling of peace and security that John gave her wasn't true love, and not the agitation and anxiety she felt when she was with Pedro. With a real effort, she pulled away from John and left the room.

"Tita, come here! I told you to take this away!"

"Doña Elena, please don't move, you'll hurt yourself. I'll remove the tray, but tell me, don't you want to eat?"

Mama Elena asked the doctor to lock the door and

confided to him her suspicions about the bitterness of the food. John replied that it might be the effect of the medicines she was taking.

"Certainly not, Doctor, if it were the medicine, I would have this taste in my mouth all of the time and I don't. They're putting something in my food—curiously enough, just since Tita came back. I want you to test it."

With a smile at her malicious insinuation, John went over to taste the ox-tail soup that had been left untouched on the tray.

"Let's see, let's find out what they've put into your food. Mmmmm! Delicious. It has beans, potatoes, chile, and . . . I can't tell very well . . . some type of meat."

"Don't play games with me. You don't notice a bitter taste?"

"No, doña Elena, not at all. But if you wish, I will send it to be analyzed. I don't want you to worry. But until they give me the results, you have to eat."

"Then get me a good cook."

"Oh, but you already have the best one right here. I understand that your daughter Tita is an exceptional cook. Some day I'm going to come and ask you for her hand."

"You know that she can't marry!" she exclaimed, gripped by a violent agitation.

John kept quiet. It didn't suit him to inflame Mama Elena. There was no point, for he had resolved to marry Tita with or without Mama Elena's permission. He knew too that Tita was no longer so concerned about that absurd destiny of hers and that as soon as she was eighteen years old, they would get married. He pronounced the visit over, ordering rest for Mama Elena, and promising to send her a new cook the next day. And so he did, but Mama Elena didn't even see fit to receive her. The doctor's remark about asking for Tita's hand had opened her eyes.

Clearly a romance had sprung up between those two.

For some time she had suspected that Tita would like to see her vanish from this earth so she would be free to wed, not just once but a thousand times if she felt like it. Mama Elena perceived this desire as a constant presence between them, in every little conversation, in every word, in every glance. But now there couldn't be the slightest doubt that Tita intended to poison her slowly in order to marry Dr. Brown. From that day on, she absolutely refused to eat anything that Tita had cooked. She ordered Chencha to take charge of the preparation of her meals. Chencha and no one else could serve it, and she had to taste the food in Mama Elena's presence before Mama Elena would make up her mind to eat it.

This new arrangement didn't bother Tita, it was a relief to delegate to Chencha the painful duty of caring for her mother, so that she was free to start embroidering the bedsheets for her trousseau. She had decided to marry John as soon as her mother was better.

The one who really suffered was Chencha. She was still recovering physically and mentally from the brutal attack that had been made on her. And although it might have seemed she would benefit from not having to do any other work than cooking and serving Mama Elena, it wasn't so. At first she received the news with pleasure, but once the shouts and reproaches started, she realized that you can't have a slice without paying for the loaf.

One day Chencha went to Dr. John Brown to have

the stitches removed where she had been torn when she was raped, and Tita fixed the meal in her place.

They thought they'd have no problem fooling Mama Elena. When she got back, Chencha served the meal and tasted it as she always did, but when Mama Elena was given some of it to eat, she immediately detected a bitter taste. Furious, she threw the tray on the floor and ordered Chencha out of the house, for having tried to deceive her.

Chencha used that excuse to spend a few days in town. She needed to forget the whole business, the rape and Mama Elena. Tita tried to convince her not to pay her mother any mind; she'd known her for years and she knew pretty well how to manage her.

"Yes, child, but why should I want to add any more bitterness to the mole I've got! Let me go, don't make trouble."

Tita held her and comforted her as she had every night since her return. She couldn't see any way to draw Chencha out of her depression, to dissuade her from the belief that no one would marry her after the violent attack she had suffered at the hands of the bandits.

"You know how men are. They all say they won't eat off a plate that isn't clean."

Seeing how desperate she was, Tita decided to let her go. She knew from experience that if Chencha stayed on the ranch near her mother, she would never be saved. Only distance would allow her to heal. The following day she sent Chencha to the village with Nicholas.

Tita found she had to hire a cook. The cook quit after three days. She couldn't stand Mama Elena's demands and her terrible manners. They hired another, who only lasted two days, and another, and another, until there was no one in the village who hadn't worked at their house. The one who lasted the longest was a deaf-mute: she put up with it for fifteen days, but she left when Mama Elena told her in signs that she was an idiot.

After that, there was nothing Mama Elena could do except eat what Tita cooked, but she took every possible precaution about it. Besides insisting that Tita taste the food in front of her, she always had a glass of warm milk brought to her with her meals, and she would drink that before eating the food, to counteract the effects of the bitter poison that according to her was dissolved in the food. Sometimes these measures alone sufficed, but occasionally she felt sharp pains in her belly, and then she took, in addition, a swig of syrup of ipecac and another of squill onion as a purgative. That did not last long. Mama Elena died within a month, wracked by horrible pains accompanied by spasms and violent convulsions. At first, Tita and John had no explanation for this strange death, since clinically Mama Elena had no other malady than her paralysis. But going through her bureau, they found the bottle of syrup of ipecac and they deduced that Mama Elena must have been taking it secretly. John informed Tita that it was a very strong emetic that could cause death.

Tita couldn't take her eyes from her mother's face during the wake. Only now, after her death, she saw her as she was for the first time and began to understand her. Anyone looking at Tita could easily have mistaken this look of recognition for a look of sorrow, but she didn't feel any sorrow. Now she finally understood the meaning of the expression "fresh as a head of lettuce"—that's the

odd, detached way a lettuce should feel at being separated abruptly from another lettuce with which it had
grown up. It would be illogical to expect it to feel pain at
this separation from another lettuce with which it had
never spoken, nor established any type of communication, and which it only knew from its outer leaves, unaware that there were many others hidden inside it.

She could not imagine that mouth with its bitter ric-
tus passionately kissing someone, nor those yellowing
cheeks flushed pink from the heat of a night of love.
Still, it had happened once. Tita had discovered it too
late and entirely by accident. Dressing her for the wake,
Tita had removed from her belt the enormous keyring
that had been chained to her as long as Tita could remember. Everything in the house was under lock and
key, strictly monitored. No one could take so much as a
cup of sugar from the pantry without Mama Elena's au-
thorization. Tita recognized the keys for all the doors
and nooks and crannies. But in addition to that enormous
keyring, Mama Elena had a little heart-shaped locket
hung around her neck, and inside it a tiny key caught
Tita's attention.

She knew immediately which lock that key fit. As a
child, playing hide-and-seek one day, she had hidden in
Mama Elena's wardrobe. Tucked among the sheets, she
had found a little box. While she waited for them to find
her, she had tried to open it, but it was locked and she
couldn't. Mama Elena hadn't been playing, she wasn't
one of the seekers, yet she was the one who discovered
Tita by opening her wardrobe door. Mama Elena had
come to get a sheet or something and had caught Tita
red-handed. Tita was punished in the cornloft, where she

had to take the kernels off a hundred ears of corn. Tita had felt that the punishment didn't fit the crime, hiding with your shoes on among the clean sheets wasn't that bad. Now, with her mother dead, reading the letters contained in the box, she realized she hadn't been punished for that, but for having tried to see what was in the box, which was serious indeed.

Full of morbid curiosity, Tita opened the box. It contained a diary and a packet of letters written to Mama Elena from someone named José Treviño. Tita put them in order by date and learned the true story of her mother's love. José was the love of her life. She hadn't been allowed to marry him because he had Negro blood in his veins. A colony of Negroes, fleeing from the Civil War in the United States, from the risk they ran of being lynched, had come to settle near the village. Young José Treviño was the product of an illicit love affair between the elder José Treviño and a beautiful Negress. When Mama Elena's parents discovered the love that existed between their daughter and this mulatto, they were horrified and forced her into an immediate marriage with Juan De la Garza, Tita's father.

This action didn't succeed in stopping her from keeping up a secret correspondence with José even after she was married, and it seemed that they hadn't limited themselves to that form of communication either, since according to the letters, Gertrudis was José's child and not her father's.

When she found out she was pregnant, Mama Elena had planned to run away with José. But, while she was waiting for him to appear that night, hidden in the darkness of the balcony, who should appear out of the shad-

ows but an unknown man who attacked José for no ap-
parent reason, eliminating him from this world. After
that terrible grief, Mama Elena resigned herself to life
with her legal husband. Though for many years Juan De
la Garza had been unaware of the entire story, he had
learned of it just when Tita was born. He had gone to a
bar to celebrate the birth of his new daughter with some
friends; there a venomous tongue had let out the information. The terrible news brought on a heart attack.
That was all there was.

Tita felt guilty for having discovered her mother's
secret. She didn't know what to do with the letters. She
thought of burning them but she was not the one to do
that; if her mother had not dared, how could she? She
put everything away just as she had found it, back in its
place.

During the funeral Tita really wept for her mother.
Not for the castrating mother who had repressed Tita
her entire life, but for the person who had lived a frustrated love. And she swore in front of Mama Elena's
tomb that come what may, she would never renounce
love. At that moment she was convinced that John, who
was always at her side supporting her without reserva-
tion, was her true love. But then she saw a group of
people approaching the mausoleum and from a distance
she made out Pedro's silhouette, and Rosaura with him,
and she was no longer so sure of her feelings.

Rosaura, displaying an enormous pregnant belly, was
walking slowly. Seeing Tita, she went and embraced her,
crying inconsolably. Pedro approached her in his turn.
When Pedro took her in his arms her body quivered like
jelly. Tita blessed her mother for providing the occasion

for her to see and embrace Pedro. Then she pulled away sharply. Pedro didn't deserve to have her love him so much. He had shown weakness by going away and leaving her; she could not forgive him.

John took Tita's hand on the way back to the ranch, and Tita in turn took his arm, to emphasize that there was something more than friendship between them. She wanted to cause Pedro the same pain she had always felt seeing him beside her sister.

Pedro watched them through slits of eyes. He didn't care a bit for the familiar way John drew near Tita when she whispered something in his ear. What was going on? Tita belonged to him, and he wasn't going to let anyone take her away. Especially not now that Mama Elena, the major obstacle to their union, had disappeared.

TO BE CONTINUED . . .

Next month's recipe:

Champandongo

CHAPTER EIGHT

AUGUST

Champandongo

INGREDIENTS:

1/4 kilo ground beef
1/4 kilo ground pork
200 grams walnuts
200 grams almonds
1 onion
1 candied citron
2 tomatoes
1 tablespoon sugar
1/4 cup cream
1/4 kilo queso manchego
1/4 cup mole
cumin
chicken stock
corn tortillas
oil

PREPARATION:

The onion is finely chopped and fried in a little oil with the meat. While it is frying, the ground cumin and a tablespoon of sugar are added.

As usual, Tita was crying as she chopped the onion. The tears clouded her vision so completely that before she realized it she cut her finger with the knife. She gave an angry cry and went back to preparing the champandongo as if nothing had happened. Right now she didn't even have a second to take care of her wound. That evening John was coming to ask for her hand, and she had to prepare a good supper in only half an hour. Tita didn't like to have to hurry with her cooking.

She always allowed enough time to cook food perfectly, trying to organize her activities in such a way that she had the peacefulness she needed in the kitchen to be able to prepare succulent dishes exactly as they should be prepared. Now she was so late that her movements were jerky and hasty, which led to that sort of accident.

The main cause of her lateness was her adorable niece, who had been born three months before, prematurely, just like Tita. The death of her mother affected Rosaura so deeply that it brought on the birth of her daughter and made nursing the child an impossibility. This time Tita couldn't or wouldn't take on the role of wet nurse, as she'd done with her nephew, and what's more, she didn't even try, perhaps because of the devastating experience she'd had when they took the child from her. Now she knew better than to establish such an intense relationship with a child who wasn't her own.

She chose instead to provide Esperanza with the same diet Nacha had used with her when she was a tiny baby: gruels and teas.

She was baptized Esperanza at Tita's request. Pedro had insisted that the child should be given the same name as Tita, Josefita. But Tita refused to hear of it. She didn't want her name to influence the child's destiny. It was enough that while giving birth to her, her mother had had a series of setbacks that forced John to perform an urgent operation that saved her life but made it impossible for her to get pregnant again.

John had explained to Tita that sometimes, because of abnormalities, the placenta does not just implant in the uterus, it sends roots down into it, so that when the baby is born, the placenta does not detach. It is so firmly attached that if an inexperienced person tried to help the mother and pulled on the placenta by yanking the umbilical cord, the whole uterus would come with it. Then it would be necessary to perform an emergency operation, removing the uterus and leaving the woman unable to become pregnant for the rest of her life.

Rosaura required surgery not because John lacked experience, but because he had no other way to loosen the placenta. And so Esperanza would be the only child, the youngest child, and, worst of all, a girl! Which meant, in the family tradition, that she was the one designated to care for her mother until the end of her days. Perhaps Esperanza sank roots in her mother's womb because she knew beforehand what to expect in this world. Tita prayed that the idea of perpetuating this cruel tradition would not cross Rosaura's mind.

To help keep that from happening, she didn't want to give her any ideas with the name, so she pressed them day and night until they agreed to call her Esperanza.

But several coincidences suggested that this child's fate would be similar to Tita's; for example, out of sheer necessity she spent the greatest part of the day in the kitchen, since her mother couldn't take care of her and her aunt could only take care of her in the kitchen, and with the gruels and the teas she was growing healthier among the tastes and smells of this warm, paradisical place.

That arrangement did not sit well with Rosaura, who felt that Tita was keeping the child away from her too much; once she had completely recovered from the operation, she asked that Esperanza be fed and brought back to her room to sleep, next to Rosaura's bed where she belonged. But that command came too late, for by then the child was used to being in the kitchen and it wasn't easy to get her out of it. She cried very, very loudly when she sensed that the warmth of the stove was no longer nearby, to such a point that Tita had to carry the stew she was cooking up to the bedroom, so they could fool the child, who was lulled to sleep by the smell and sensation of warmth from the pan Tita was using for cooking. Then Tita carried the enormous pan back to the kitchen and went on preparing the meal.

But today the child had outshone herself. Perhaps she sensed that her aunt was thinking of getting married and departing the ranch, leaving her behind all adrift, for all day long she never stopped crying. Tita ran up and down the stairs carrying pots of food from one end to the other. Finally it just had to happen: *the pitcher went to the well once too often.* Going down the stairs for the eighth time, Tita tripped and the pan full of mole for the champandongo rolled down the steps. And with it went four hours of hard work cutting and grinding ingredients.

Putting her hands to her head, Tita sat down on the step and tried to catch her breath. She had been up since five that morning to keep from hurrying, and it had all been for nothing. She would have to start over preparing the mole.

Pedro couldn't have chosen a worse moment to speak to Tita, but seeing her on the stairs, apparently resting, he went over to try to convince her that she shouldn't marry John.

"Tita, I want to say, I think your idea of marrying John is a terrible mistake. There's still time, don't make this mistake, please, don't agree to the marriage!"

"Pedro, you're hardly the one to tell me what I should or shouldn't do. When you were going to get married, I didn't ask you not to do it, even though your wedding destroyed me. You have your life, now leave me in peace to have mine!"

"It's because of just that decision, which I repent wholeheartedly, that I'm asking you to reconsider. You know quite well what the motive was that joined me to your sister, but it turned out to be a pointless act, it didn't work, and now I think it would have been better to run away with you."

"Well, you think so too late. Nothing can be done about it now. I entreat you, never bother me again for the rest of my life, and don't ever dare to repeat what you've just said to me, my sister might hear it and we don't need one more unhappy person in this house. Excuse me! . . . Ah, and let me suggest, next time you fall in love, don't be such a coward!"

Picking up the pan angrily, Tita went into the kitchen. Between her muttering and shoving dishes around, she finished the mole; as it cooked, she went on with the preparation of the champandongo.

When the meat starts to brown, the chopped tomato is added, along with the citron, the walnuts, and the almonds, cut into small pieces.

The steam rising from the pan mingled with the heat given off by Tita's body. The anger she felt within her acted like yeast on bread dough. She felt its rapid rising, flowing into every last recess of her body; like yeast in a small bowl, it spilled over to the outside, escaping in the form of steam through her ears, nose, and all her pores.

A small part of this boundless fury was caused by her discussion with Pedro, another part by her accidents and her work in the kitchen, and the largest part by something Rosaura had said a few days before. Tita, John, and Alex had been together in her sister's bedroom. John had brought his son along on his medical call because the boy missed having Tita in the house and wanted to see her again. He stuck his face up to the cradle to see Esperanza and was struck by the girl's beauty. Like all children his age, he didn't have any secrets, and he declaimed:

"Papa, I want to get married too, just like you. With this little girl."

They all laughed at that, but when Rosaura explained to Alex that he couldn't because this little girl was destined to take care of her until the day she died, Tita felt her hair stand on end. Only Rosaura could have thought to perpetuate such an inhuman tradition.

If only Rosaura had burned her mouth to a crisp! And had never let those words leak out, those foul, filthy, frightful, repulsive, revolting, unreasonable words. Better to have swallowed them and kept them deep in her bowels until they were putrid and worm-eaten. If only she would live long enough to prevent her sister from carrying out such a dire intention.

She didn't know why she had to think about such unpleasant things at a time like this, which was supposed to be the happiest time of her life, nor why she had to feel so irritable. Perhaps Pedro had infected her with his bad temper. Since they returned to the ranch and he found out that Tita was thinking of marrying John, he had been possessed by the furies. You couldn't say so much as a word to him. He went out very early and rode around the ranch, his horse at a gallop. He returned at nightfall, just in time for supper, and shut himself in his room immediately afterward.

Nobody had an explanation for his behavior; some believed the thought of not having any more children hurt him deeply. Whatever it was, it seemed his rage dominated the thoughts and actions of everyone in the house. Tita was literally "like water for chocolate"—she was on the verge of boiling over. How irritable she was! Even the cooing she loved so much—the sound made by the doves she had reestablished under the roof of the house, a sound that had given her so much pleasure since her return—even that noise was annoying. She felt her head about to burst, like a kernel of popcorn. To prevent that from happening, she pressed both her hands against it hard. A timid tap on her shoulder made her jump; she felt an urge to punch whoever it was, surely someone who wanted to take up more of her time. What a surprise it was to see Chencha standing in front of her. The Chencha of old, smiling and happy. Never in her life had Tita been so delighted to see her, not even when Chencha had visited her in John's house. As usual Chencha had dropped from the sky just when Tita needed her most.

It was amazing to see the recovery Chencha had made, after the state of misery and despair in which she had left.

No signs remained of the trauma she had suffered. The man who had managed to erase them was standing at her side, with a huge honest smile on his face. From a distance, Tita could tell she was dealing with a decent, quiet man; though Chencha didn't let him open his mouth any farther than to say "Jesús Martinez at your service." After that, Chencha monopolized the conversation completely, as usual, and broke a speed record bringing Tita up to date on the events in her life:

Jesús had been her first sweetheart, and he had never forgotten her. Chencha's folks had been flatly opposed to their romance, and he never would have known where to find her if it hadn't been for Chencha's going back to the village and his coming to see her. It didn't matter to him that Chencha wasn't a virgin; he married her right away. Now that Mama Elena was dead, they were coming to the ranch together, with the idea of starting a new life and having lots of children and being very happy for ever and ever. . . .

Chencha stopped for breath since she was turning purple and Tita took advantage of the interruption to tell her—not talking as fast as her, but nearly—how pleased she was that she had returned to the ranch; tomorrow they would discuss the terms of Jesús's employment, today John was coming to ask for her hand, pretty soon she'd be married, but she still hadn't finished the supper. Could Chencha take over so she could take a cool, soothing bath and be presentable when John arrived, any minute now?

Chencha promptly took charge, practically throwing Tita out of the kitchen. She could make champandongo, she said, with her eyes closed and her hands tied.

After the meat has been cooked and drained, the next step is to fry the tortillas in oil, lightly, so they don't get hard. In the dish destined for the oven, spread a layer of cream so the other ingredients don't stick, a layer of tortillas, and over these a layer of the ground meat mixture, and finally the mole, covering it with the sliced cheese, and the cream. Repeat this process as many times as necessary until the pan is filled. Put the pan in the oven and bake until the cheese melts and the tortillas are softened. Serve with rice and beans.

What peace of mind it gave Tita to know that Chencha was in the kitchen. Now all she had to worry about was getting herself ready. She swept across the patio like a gust of wind to start to bathe. She could count only as much as ten minutes to bathe and get dressed, put on perfume, and do her hair adequately. She was in such a hurry that she didn't even see Pedro, at the far end of the patio, kicking stones.

Tita stripped off her clothes, got into the shower, and let the cold water fall on her. What a relief! With her eyes closed, her senses were more acute, so she could feel each drop of cold water that ran down her body. She felt her nipples grow hard as stone when the water touched them. Another stream of water ran down her back and curved like a waterfall over the round thrust of her buttocks, flowing down her firm legs to her feet. Little by little, her bad mood was passing, and her head-ache was going away. Suddenly the water started to feel warmer and it kept getting warmer and warmer until it began to burn her skin. This sometimes happened when it was hot outside, after the powerful rays of the sun had been heating the water in the tank all day, but this wasn't possible now since, first of all, it wasn't summer and sec-ond, it was starting to get dark. Alarmed, she opened her eyes, afraid that the bathroom was on fire again, and what did she see on the other side of the planks but Pedro, watching her intently.

The way Pedro's eyes were shining, it was impossible not to see them in the shadows, the way two tiny drops of dew, hidden in the weeds, can't remain unnoticed when they are struck by the first rays of the sun. Damn Pedro's eyes! Damn the carpenter who rebuilt the bathroom so it was just like the previous one, with spaces between each and every board. When Tita saw that Pedro was approaching her, with lust in his eyes, she went running out of the bathroom, throwing her clothes on any which way. As fast as she could, she ran to her room and shut the door.

She barely had time to finish getting dressed, before Chencha came to announce that John had just arrived and was waiting in the living room.

She couldn't go receive him immediately, since the table still hadn't been laid. Before putting down the tablecloth, it's necessary to protect the table with a table cover, so that the glasses and dishes don't make any noise when they strike it. It should be a white baize one, so the whiteness of the tablecloth is intensified. Tita gently slid it across an enormous table that seated twenty people, one that was only used on occasions like this. She was trying not to make any noise, not even to breathe, so she could hear what Rosaura, Pedro, and John were saying in the living room. The dining and living rooms were separated by a long hall; the only sound that came to Tita was the low murmur of men's voices, Pedro and John's, but she could tell from the tone of their voices that they were arguing. Instead of waiting for matters to develop, she moved quickly to put the plates, the plate covers, the glasses, the saltcellars, and the knifeholders in their proper places on the table.

Without pausing, she put the candles under the platewarmers that would hold the first, middle, and main courses and left them sitting ready on the sideboard. She ran to the kitchen for the Bordeaux wine that she had left in a bain-marie. Bordeaux wines should be taken from the wine cellar several hours in advance and put in a warm spot so the gentle warming develops the flavor, but since Tita had forgotten to take it out on time, she was forced to resort to this artificial method. The only thing remaining was to place a small basket of flowers in the center of the table—but in order to preserve the natural freshness of the flowers, they should not be arranged until just before the guests are to be seated, so Tita assigned that task to Chencha; hurriedly, at least as much as her starched dress allowed, she made her way to the living room.

The first sight that presented itself when she opened the door was Pedro and John in heated discussion about the political situation of the country. It appeared that the two of them had forgotten the most elementary rules of good manners, which tell us that at a social gathering one does not bring up the subject of personalities, sad topics or unfortunate facts, religion, or politics. Tita's entrance stopped the discussion and forced them to try to begin a conversation in a more amicable tone.

In this tense atmosphere, John advanced his petition for Tita's hand. Pedro, as the man of the house, sullenly gave his approval. They started to work out the details. When they tried to fix the date for the wedding, Tita learned of John's desire to delay it for a while so he could make a trip to the northern part of the United States to bring back his only living aunt, whom he wanted to attend the ceremony. This presented a serious problem for Tita: she wanted to get away from the ranch—and the proximity of Pedro—as quickly as possible.

To formalize their engagement, John handed Tita a beautiful diamond ring. Tita looked at it for a long time, shining on her finger. The glints of light it gave off reminded her of the gleam in Pedro's eyes a short time ago, when he was watching her naked, and a poem that Nacha had taught her as a child came into her head:

> *The sun lights up a drop of dew*
> *The drop of dew soon dries*
> *You are the light of my eyes, my eyes*
> *I'm brought to life by you . . .*

Rosaura was moved by the tears in her sister's eyes, taking them for tears of joy, and she felt a slight lifting of the guilt she sometimes suffered for having married Tita's sweetheart. Then, quite enthused, she poured them each a glass of champagne and called for a toast, to the happiness of the engaged couple. When all four of them gathered together in the center of the living room to drink the toast, Pedro clinked his glass so violently against the others' that it broke into a thousand pieces and their champagne was splashed onto their clothes and faces.

It was a blessing that Chencha appeared at this very moment, amid the reigning confusion, and pronounced those magical words *supper is served.* That announcement restored the calm and the good cheer that the occasion warranted but that they had been on the point of losing. When the talk turns to eating, a subject of the greatest importance, only fools and sick men don't give it the attention it deserves. And, that not being the case here, in a fine mood, they all made their way to the dining room.

During supper everything went very smoothly, thanks to the graceful intervention Chencha provided while serving. The meal wasn't as delicious as on some other occasions, perhaps because of the bad temper Tita was in while she prepared it, but neither could you say it wasn't pleasant. Champandongo is a dish with such a refined flavor that no temper can be bad enough to ruin its enjoyment. When they had finished, Tita walked John to the door and there gave him a big farewell kiss. John was thinking of leaving the following day, so that he could come back as soon as possible.

Returning to the kitchen, Tita thanked Chencha for the great help she'd been and then sent her to clean the room and the mattress she would be using with her husband Jesús. Before getting into bed, they had to make sure they wouldn't discover the undesirable presence of bedbugs in their room. The last servant who had slept there had left it infested with those little creatures and Tita had not been able to disinfect it because of the hard work that followed the birth of Rosaura's daughter.

The best way to eradicate them is to mix a glass of alcohol, half an ounce of spirits of turpentine, and half an ounce of powdered camphor. Rub this preparation everywhere there are bedbugs, and they will disappear completely.

Withdrawing to the kitchen, Tita began putting the pots and pans away. She still wasn't sleepy, and it was better to spend the time this way than tossing and turning in her bed. She felt a mass of conflicting emotions and the best way to put some order in her thoughts was to start by putting some order in the kitchen. She took a huge earthenware pot and put it away in what was now the storage room, formerly the dark room. After Mama Elena's death they saw that no one was thinking of using it as a place to bathe, since they all preferred to use the shower, so to put it to some use they turned it into a storeroom for kitchen utensils.

In one hand she was carrying the pot, in the other, an oil lamp. She pushed her way into the storeroom, trying not to trip on all the things that stood in her path, the many cooking pans that were kept there because they were not often used. The light from the lamp helped a little, but not enough—it didn't reveal the shadow that slipped silently into the room behind her and shut the door.

Sensing another's presence, Tita spun around; the light clearly revealed the figure of Pedro, barring the door.

"Pedro! What are you doing here?"

Without answering, Pedro went to her, extinguished the lamp, pulled her to a brass bed that had once belonged to her sister Gertrudis, and throwing himself upon her, caused her to lose her virginity and learn of true love.

In her bedroom, Rosaura was trying to put her daughter to sleep, but the baby was crying uncontrollably. She was walking her all around the room, but it wasn't working. As she walked past the window, she saw a strange glow coming from the dark room. Plumes of phosphorescent colors were ascending to the sky like delicate Bengal lights. As many cries of alarm as she gave, calling for Tita and Pedro to come see, the only answer she got was from Chencha, who was looking for a set of sheets. Beholding this remarkable sight, Chencha was struck dumb with surprise for the first time in her life; not a single sound escaped her lips. Esperanza, who was always keenly aware of what went on around her, stopped her crying. Chencha knelt and crossed herself and offered up a prayer.

"Most holy Virgin, who's up in heaven, gather up the soul of my mistriss Elena an' let her stop wandering among the shades in pulgatory!"

"What are you saying, Chencha, what are you talking about?"

"What else can it be, can't you see it's a ghost of the dead! Dead and still walking, paying for some unsettled score! I don't think it's no joke, I'm never going nowhere near it!"

"Me neither."

If poor Mama Elena had known that even after she was dead her presence was enough to inspire terror—and that this fear of encountering her is what provided Tita and Pedro the perfect opportunity to profane her favorite place with impunity, rolling voluptuously on Gertrudis's bed—she would have died another hundred times over.

TO BE CONTINUED . . .

Next month's recipe:

Chocolate and Three Kings' Day Bread

CHAPTER NINE

SEPTEMBER

*Chocolate and Three
Kings' Day Bread*

INGREDIENTS FOR THE CHOCOLATE:

2 pounds Soconusco chocolate
 beans
2 pounds Maracaibo chocolate
 beans
2 pounds Caracas chocolate
 beans
4 to 6 pounds sugar, to taste

PREPARATION:

The first step is to toast the chocolate beans. It's good to use a metal pan rather than an earthenware griddle since the pores of the griddle soak up the oil the beans give off. It's very important to pay attention to this sort of detail, since the goodness of the chocolate depends on three things, namely: that the chocolate beans used are good and without defect, that you mix several different types of beans to make the chocolate, and, finally, the amount of toasting.

It's advisable to toast the cocoa beans just until the moment they begin to give off oil. If they are removed from the heat before then, they will make a discolored and disagreeable-looking chocolate, which will be indigestible besides. On the other hand, if they are left on the heat too long, most of the beans will be burned, which will make the chocolate bitter and acrid.

Tita extracted just half a teaspoon of this oil to mix

with sweet almond oil for an excellent lip ointment. Her lips always chapped every winter, no matter what precautions she took. When she was a child, this caused her considerable discomfort; whenever she laughed the fleshy part of her lips would crack open and bleed, producing a sharp pain. In time she grew resigned to this. Now that she didn't have a lot of reasons to laugh, it no longer concerned her. She could wait patiently for spring for the cracks to disappear. The only reason she was making the pomade was that some guests were coming to the house tonight to share the Kings' Day bread.

It was for vanity that she wanted her lips to look soft and shiny for the party, not because she expected to laugh very much. The suspicion that she was pregnant hardly brought a laugh to her lips! This possibility had not occurred to her as she consummated her love with Pedro. She still hadn't told him. She planned to do so tonight, but she didn't know how. What would Pedro's reaction be? And the solution to this huge problem? She had no idea.

She would rather not torment herself, would rather turn her mind toward more trivial matters like the preparation of a good lip balm. For that there's nothing like cocoa butter. But before starting to prepare it, she had to have the chocolate ready.

When the cocoa beans are done being toasted, as described above, they are cleaned using a hair sieve to separate the hull from the bean. Beneath the metate in which the chocolate is to be ground place a flat pan containing a hot fire; once the stone is warm, begin grinding the chocolate. Mix the chocolate with the sugar, pounding it with a mallet and grinding the two together. Then divide the mixture into chunks. The chunks are shaped by hand into tablets, square or round, according to your preference, and set out to air. The dividing points can be marked with the tip of a knife if you wish.

While Tita was forming the squares, she mourned for the Three Kings' days of her childhood, when she didn't have such serious problems. Her biggest worry then was that the Magi never brought her what she asked for, but instead what Mama Elena thought best for her. It was some years before she learned the reason she had received the longed-for gift on one occasion; Nacha had saved up her wages for a long time to buy her the "little movie" she had seen in the display window of a store. It was called a little movie, because it was an apparatus for projecting images on the wall using a petroleum lamp as a light source, producing an effect like a movie; but its real name was "zoetrope." What joy she felt seeing it next to her stocking when she got up in the morning. How she and her sisters enjoyed the many afternoons spent watching the sequence of images drawn on strips of glass, which pictured different situations that were so entertaining. Those happy days when Nacha was with her seemed so distant now. Nacha! The smells: her noodle soup, her chilaquiles, her champurrado, her molcajete sauce, her bread with cream, all were far away in a distant past. They could never be surpassed, her seasoning, her atole drinks, her teas, her laugh, her herbal remedies, the way she braided her hair and tucked Tita in at night, took care of her when she was sick, and cooked what she craved and whipped the chocolate! If she could bring back a single moment from that time, a little of the happiness from those days, she could prepare the Kings' Day bread with the same enthusiasm she had felt then! If only she could eat the bread afterward with her sisters, laughing and joking, just like old times, when she and Rosaura had not had to compete for the love of a man, before she knew that she would not be allowed to wed, that Gertrudis would run away from home and work in a brothel, and when she still believed that if she found the doll in the bread, all her wishes would miraculously come true, literally, everything she had wished for. Life had taught her that it was not that easy; there are few prepared to fulfill their desires whatever the cost, and the right to determine the course of one's own life would take more effort than she had imagined. That battle she had to fight alone, and it weighed on her. If she could only have her sister Gertrudis by her side! But it seemed more likely that a corpse would come back to life than that Gertrudis would come back home.

No one had gone for news of her since Nicholas had taken her clothes to the brothel. Putting those memories to rest along with the squares of chocolate she had just finished, Tita began the Three Kings' Day bread at last.

INGREDIENTS:

30 grams fresh yeast
1 1/4 kilos flour
8 eggs
1 tablespoon salt
2 tablespoons orange-blossom water
1 1/2 cups milk
300 grams sugar
300 grams butter

250 grams candied fruit
1 porcelain doll

PREPARATION:

Break up the yeast in 1/4 kilo of flour using your hands or a fork and adding 1/2 cup of warm milk a little at a time. When the ingredients are well blended, knead briefly, form into a ball, and let rest, until the dough grows to double its size.

Just as Tita was putting the dough to rest, Rosaura made her appearance in the kitchen. She came to ask Tita's help in carrying out the diet John had prescribed for her. For some weeks now, she had been having serious digestive problems, she suffered from flatulence and bad breath. Rosaura felt so distressed by these upheavals that she had determined that she and Pedro should sleep in separate bedrooms. That reduced her suffering slightly; she could pass gas as she pleased. John had recommended that she abstain from such foods as root and leafy vegetables, and that she perform some active physical labor. This last was made difficult by her excessive bulk. There was no explaining the way she had gotten so fat after her return to the ranch, since she was still eating the same as always. It took an enormous effort for her to set her voluminous, gelatinous body in motion. All these ills carried with them an infinity of problems, the worst being that every day Pedro moved farther and farther away from her. She couldn't blame him; even she couldn't stand the foul smell. She couldn't take any more.

It was the first time Rosaura had plucked up her courage and discussed these topics with Tita. She confessed

she had not approached her before because of the jealousy she felt. She had thought that there was an amorous
relationship between Tita and Pedro, concealed, hidden
by outward appearances. Now that she saw how much
John loved her, and how soon she would be married to
him, she had realized the absurdity of continuing to harbor this type of suspicion. She was sure there was still
time to establish good relations between them. To tell
the truth, until now the Rosaura-Tita relationship had
been like water in boiling oil! With tears in her eyes, she
begged Tita not to harbor bad feelings about her marriage to Pedro. She asked Tita's advice how to save it. As
if Tita was the one to dispense that kind of advice! With
difficulty, Rosaura reported that it had been several
months since Pedro had approached her with amorous
intentions. He practically avoided her. That alone didn't
worry her too much; Pedro had never been disposed to
sexual excess. It wasn't just that, it was his attitude—in it
she detected his frank rejection of her.

And she could put her finger on just when it started,
since she remembered perfectly. It was the night the
ghost of Mama Elena first appeared. She was awake,
waiting for Pedro to return from his walk. When he returned, he paid almost no attention to her story of the
ghost, as if he was hardly there. During the night she
had tried to embrace him, but he was either asleep or
pretending to be, and he didn't respond to her advances.
Later she had heard him weeping quietly; then she had
pretended not to hear.

She felt sure that her fatness, her flatulence, and her
foul breath were driving Pedro farther away every day,

and she couldn't see a solution. So now she was asking Tita's help. She needed help as never before; she had no one else to turn to. Every day the situation grew more serious. She didn't know how she would react to what "they" would say if Pedro left her, she couldn't stand it. Her only consolation was that at least she had her daughter Esperanza, who was obliged to stay with her forever.

Until that point all was going well, since what Rosaura said had produced pangs in Tita's conscience, but when she heard for the second time what Esperanza's fate was to be, she had to make a supreme effort not to shout at her sister that it was the sickest idea she had heard in her life. She couldn't begin a discussion between them right now that would spoil the good impulse she felt to forgive Rosaura for how she had harmed her. Instead of voicing her thoughts, Tita promised her sister that she would prepare a special diet to help her lose weight. She kindly supplied her with a family remedy against bad breath: "Bad breath originates in the stomach and several causes contribute to it. To eliminate it, start by gargling salt water mixed with a few drops of powdered camphor vinegar, sniffing the mixture up into the nostrils at the same time. In addition, chew mint leaves constantly. By itself, the regimen proposed here, when followed rigorously, can purify the foulest breath."

Rosaura was infinitely grateful for her sister's help and quickly went out to the garden to pick some mint leaves, asking for Tita's absolute discretion in this delicate matter. But Tita was distraught. What had she done! How could she make up for the harm she'd done to

Rosaura, to Pedro, to herself, to John? How could she face him when she saw him in a few days, when he returned from his trip? John, the person to whom she owed nothing but thanks; John, who had brought her back to her senses; John, who had shown her the way to freedom.

John, his peace, serenity, reason. Truly, he did not deserve this! What could she tell him, what could she do? For the moment, the best thing she could do was to continue preparing the Kings' Day bread, since the leavened dough she had left to rest while she talked with Rosaura was now ready for the next step.

Use a kilo of flour to form a well on the table. Place all the ingredients in the center of this well and begin kneading, starting in the center and gradually adding a little of the flour from the well until all the flour has been incorporated. When the leavened dough has risen to twice its size, combine it with this other dough, blending them perfectly, until the dough comes off your hands easily. Use a scraper to remove any dough that has stuck to the table, so that it can be blended in as well. Place the dough in a deep container that has been greased. Cover with a napkin and wait for it to rise until it has doubled in size yet again. Take into account the fact that it takes approximately two hours for the dough to double in size and that it has to rise three times before it is put into the oven.

As Tita was putting the napkin over the container where she had set the dough to rest, a strong gust of wind banged the kitchen door wide open, causing an icy blast to invade the room. The napkin flew into the air and an icy shiver ran down Tita's spine. She turned around and was stunned to find herself face to face with Mama Elena, who was giving her a fierce look.

"I told you many times not to go near Pedro. Why did you do it?"

"I tried, Mami . . . but . . ."

"But nothing! What you have done has no name! You have forgotten all morality, respect, and good behavior. You are worthless, a good-for-nothing who doesn't respect even yourself. You have blackened the name of my entire family, from my ancestors down to this cursed baby you carry in your belly!"

"No! My baby isn't cursed!"

"Yes, it is! I curse it! It and you, forever!"

"No, please!"

Chencha's entrance into the kitchen caused Mama Elena to spin on her heels and go out the same door by which she had entered.

"Close the door, child. Can't you feel how cold it is? Lately you've seemed so up in the air. What is bothering you?"

Nothing. Except she had missed a period and thought she was pregnant; and she had to tell John when he came back to marry her to cancel the wedding, and she had to leave the ranch if she wanted to have her baby without problems, and she had to give up Pedro forever, since she couldn't go on hurting Rosaura.

That was all! But she couldn't say that to Chencha. She was such a gossip that if Tita told her, the next day the whole village would know. She preferred to give her no answer and change the subject without more ado, much as Chencha did to her when she was caught out on some weak point.

"How awful! The dough is already rising over the pan. Let me finish the bread, or tomorrow night will catch us and we still won't be done."

The dough wasn't yet over the top of the pan where she'd put it to rest, but it was an ideal pretext to divert Chencha's attention onto another topic.

When the dough has doubled in size for the second time, remove it from the container, place it on the table, and form it into a strip. If you wish, you may place some bits of candied fruit in the middle. If not, just the porcelain doll, placed at random. Roll up the strip, joining one edge to the other. Place the bread seam down on a greased and floured baking sheet. Form a ring with the dough, leaving enough space between the ring and the edge of the baking sheet, since the dough still has to double in size one more time. Meanwhile, light the oven to maintain a comfortable temperature in the kitchen until the bread finishes rising.

Before placing the porcelain doll in the bread, Tita looked at it for a long time. Traditionally, on the night of the sixth of January, the bread is sliced and the person who finds the doll hidden inside it is required to hold a celebration on the second of February, Candlemas day, when the Baby Jesus is removed from the Nativity scene. Ever since they were very young, this tradition had been converted into a sort of competition between her and her sisters. The one lucky enough to find the doll was considered lucky indeed. That night, with the doll clasped tightly in her two hands, she could make any wish she wanted.

Carefully studying the delicate form of the doll, she

was thinking how easy it was to wish for things as a child. Then nothing seemed impossible. Growing up, one realizes how many things one cannot wish for, the things that are forbidden, sinful. Indecent.

But what is decent? To deny everything that you really want? She wished she had never grown up, never known Pedro, never had to flee from him. She wished her mother would stop tormenting her, jumping out at her from every corner and crying contempt for her behavior. She wished Esperanza could marry, without Rosaura being able to stop her, so she would never know this pain and suffering! She wished that the child would have the strength Gertrudis had shown and run away from home, if necessary! She wished Gertrudis would come home, to lend Tita the support she needed so much now! Making these wishes, she placed the doll in the bread and left the bread on the table so it could rise.

When the bread has doubled in size the third time, decorate it with candied fruit, glaze it with a beaten egg, and sprinkle it with sugar. Bake it in the oven for twenty minutes, and let it cool.

When the bread was ready to serve, Tita asked Pedro to help her carry it to the table. She could have asked anyone's help with it, but she needed to speak to him in private.

"Pedro, I need to talk to you alone."

"That's easy, why not go to the dark room? There we can do it without anyone bothering us. I've been waiting for you to come there for several days."

"Those visits to the dark room are just what I have to talk to you about."

Chencha interrupted their conversation to inform them that the Loboses had just arrived at the party, and everyone was waiting for them to cut the bread. So Tita and Pedro had no choice but to postpone their conversation and carry the bread to the dining room, where it was anxiously awaited. As they crossed the hallway, Tita saw her mother, motionless beside the door to the dining room, throwing her a furious look. She was petrified. Pulque began to bark at Mama Elena, who was walking toward Tita threateningly. The fur on the dog's back was sticking straight up from fear and he was backing away, on the defensive. In his excitement, he put his back leg into the brass spittoon that stood at the end of the hall, next to the fern, and when he tried to run away, he knocked it over, spraying its contents in every direction.

The uproar he created drew the attention of the twelve guests, who were all sitting together in the living room. Alarmed, they looked out into the hall, and Pedro was forced to explain that Pulque did this type of inexplicable thing lately, perhaps because he was getting old, but that everything was under control. Nevertheless Paquita Lobo could see that Tita was on the verge of fainting. She asked someone else to help Pedro carry the bread to the dining room, since she saw that Tita was not feeling well. She took her arm and led her to the living room. She made Tita sniff some smelling salts, and soon she had recovered completely. They then decided to go to the dining room. Before leaving, Paquita detained Tita briefly and asked:

"Are you feeling all right? I notice you still seem a little dizzy, and the look on your face! If I didn't know perfectly well that you are a decent girl, I would swear that you are pregnant."

Tita, laughing and trying to appear casual, replied to her.

"Pregnant? Only you would think of something like that! And what does the look on my face have to do with it?"

"I can tell from a woman's eyes the minute she becomes pregnant."

Tita was grateful to Pulque who again rescued her from an awkward situation, since the incredible commotion that broke out on the patio kept her from having to continue this conversation with Paquita. Besides Pulque's barking she could hear the sound of several horses galloping. All the guests were already in the house. Who could it be at this hour? Tita hurried to the door, opened it, and saw what Pulque was making such a fuss over, a person riding at the head of a band of revolutionary soldiers. When they got close enough, she could see that the person in charge of that troop was none other than her sister Gertrudis. At her side rode the man who had carried her off years ago, Juan Alejandrez, now a general. Gertrudis got down from her horse and as if no time at all had passed, said confidently that since she knew it was the day they cut the Three Kings' bread, she had come for a good cup of freshly whipped hot chocolate. Tita, deeply moved, embraced her and led her straight to the table to grant her wish. In this house they made hot chocolate like nobody else's, since they took so much care with every step in making it, from its preparation to the whipping of the chocolate, yet another critical procedure. Inexpert beating can turn an excellent-quality chocolate into a disgusting drink, either by under- or overcooking, making it too thick or even burnt.

There's a very simple method for avoiding the aforementioned problems: heat a square of chocolate in water. The amount of water used should be a little more than enough to fill the cups. When the water comes to a boil for the first time, remove it from the heat, and dissolve the chocolate completely; beat with a chocolate-mill until it is smoothly blended with the water. Return the pan to the stove. When it comes to a boil again and starts to boil over, remove it from the heat. Put it back on the heat and bring it to a boil a third time. Remove from the heat and beat the chocolate. Pour half into a little pitcher and beat the rest of it some more. Then serve it all, leaving the top covered with foam. Hot chocolate can also be made using milk instead of water, but in this case, it should only be brought to a boil once, and the second time it's heated it should be beaten so it doesn't get too thick. However, hot chocolate made with water is more digestible than that made with milk.

Gertrudis closed her eyes each time she took a sip from the cup of chocolate she had in front of her. Life would be much nicer if one could carry the smells and tastes of the maternal home wherever one pleased. Well, this was no longer her mother's house. Her mother had died without her knowing it.

She felt real grief when Tita informed her of her mother's death. She had come back with the intention of showing Mama Elena how she had triumphed in life. She was a *general* in the revolutionary army. The commission had been earned by sheer hard work, she fought like mad on the field of battle. Leadership was in her blood, and once she joined the army, she began a rapid ascent through powerful positions until she arrived at the top; moreover, she was coming back happily married to Juan. They had met after not seeing each other for more than a year and their passion had been reborn, just like the day they met. What more could a person ask! How she would have liked her mother to have seen it; how she would have liked to see her, even if only to be told with a look that she needed to wipe the traces of chocolate from her lips with her napkin.

That was chocolate prepared like it used to be.

Eyes closed, Gertrudis offered up a silent prayer, asking that Tita be granted many more years in which to prepare the family recipes. Neither she nor Rosaura knew how to make them; when Tita died, her family's past would die with her. When they had finished supper they moved to the living room and the dance began. The salon was ablaze with the light from a colossal number of candles. Juan impressed all the guests with the wonderful way he played the guitar, the harmonica, and the accordion. Gertrudis kept time to the songs Juan played, tapping the floor with the toe of her boot.

She was watching him proudly from the far end of the salon, where a court of admirers had surrounded her, besieging her with questions about her part in the revolution. Smoking a cigarette, Gertrudis, perfectly at her ease, was regaling them with fantastic stories of the battles she'd been in. She had them openmouthed, as she told them about the first firing squad she had ordered, but she couldn't contain herself. She interrupted her story and flung herself into the center of the salon where she began to dance gracefully to the polka *"Jesusita in Chihuahua,"* which Juan was playing brilliantly on the norteño accordion. She lightly hitched her skirt up to her knee, quite uninhibited.

This attitude provoked scandalized comments among the ladies gathered there.

Rosaura whispered in Tita's ear.

"I don't know where Gertrudis gets her sense of rhythm. Mama didn't like to dance, and they say Papa was very bad at it."

Tita shrugged her shoulders in answer, although she knew perfectly well who had given Gertrudis her rhythm and other qualities. That secret she planned to take to her grave; but it was not to be. A year later Gertrudis gave birth to a mulatto baby. Juan was furious and threatened to leave her. He couldn't forgive Gertrudis for having returned to her old ways. Then Tita, to save their marriage, told them everything. It was fortunate she had not dared to burn the letters, since now her mother's "black past" served to establish proof of Gertrudis's innocence.

It was a hard blow for him to take, but at least they didn't separate; instead they lived together forever and were happy more often than not.

Tita knew the reason for Gertrudis's sense of rhythm, just as she knew the reason for the failure of Rosaura's marriage and for her own pregnancy. Now what she wanted to know was the solution. That was what mattered. At least now she had someone in whom to confide her problems. She hoped that Gertrudis would stay on the ranch long enough to hear her story and give her some advice. Chencha, on the other hand, wished just the opposite. She was furious at Gertrudis; not exactly at her, but at the work involved in waiting on her troop. Instead of enjoying the party, at this hour of the night she had had to set up a huge table on the patio and prepare chocolate for the fifty men in the troop.

TO BE CONTINUED . . .

Next month's recipe:

Cream Fritters

CHAPTER TEN

OCTOBER

Cream Fritters

INGREDIENTS:

1 cup of heavy cream
6 eggs
cinnamon
syrup

PREPARATION:

Take the eggs, crack them, and separate the whites. Stir
the six yolks with the cup of cream. Beat until the mixture becomes light. Pour it into a pot that has been
greased with lard. The mixture should be no more than
an inch thick in the baking pan. Place it on the heat,
over a very low flame, and allow to thicken.

   Tita was preparing these fritters at the specific request of Gertrudis; they were her favorite dessert. It had
been a long time since she had had them, and she
wanted to make them before leaving the ranch, the next
day. Gertrudis had only been home for a week, but that
was much longer than she had intended. While she
greased the pot where Tita would pour the beaten cream,
she never stopped talking. She had so many things to tell
Tita that she could talk day and night for a month without running out of conversation. Tita listened, greatly
interested. More than interested, she was afraid to let her

stop; then it would be her turn. She knew that today was the only day she had left to tell Gertrudis about her problem, and even though she was dying to get it off her chest and confess to her sister, she was worried about what attitude Gertrudis might take with her.

Having Gertrudis and her troops staying at the house had not made Tita feel oppressed by extra work, instead it had provided her with a real peace.

With so many people around the house and the patios, it was impossible to talk to Pedro, much less meet him in the dark room. This was a relief to Tita, since she wasn't ready to talk with him. Before doing that she wanted to analyze the possible solutions to the problem of her pregnancy carefully and come to some decision. She and Pedro were on one side; on the other, at a total disadvantage, was her sister. Rosaura was weak, it was important to her how society saw her, and she was still fat and smelly; even the remedy Tita had given her had not reduced her huge problem. What would happen if Pedro abandoned her for Tita? How much would that hurt Rosaura? What about Esperanza?

"I'm boring you with my chatter, aren't I?"

"Of course not, Gertrudis. Why do you say that?"

"You've seemed distant for quite a while. Tell me, what is it? It's about Pedro, right?"

"Yes."

"If you still love him, then why are you going to marry John?"

"I'm not going to marry him, I can't."

Tita hugged Gertrudis and cried on her shoulder, without saying anything more.

Gertrudis stroked her hair tenderly, but was careful

to watch the fritter dessert that was on the flame. It would be a pity if she couldn't eat it. When it was almost starting to burn, she detached herself from Tita and said sweetly:

"Just let me take this off the burner, and then you can go right back to crying, okay?"

Tita couldn't keep back a smile that Gertrudis seemed more worried about the future of the fritters at the moment than about Tita's. That was understandable, for Gertrudis was unaware of the seriousness of her sister's problem; and she had a strong craving for fritters.

Drying her tears, Tita removed the pan from the heat herself, since Gertrudis burned her hand trying to do it.

Once the custard is cool, it is cut into small squares, a size that won't crumble too easily. Next the egg whites are beaten, so the squares of custard can be rolled in them and fried in oil. Finally, the fritters are served in syrup and sprinkled with ground cinnamon.

While they let the custard cool so it could weather the storm to come, Tita confided all her problems in Gertrudis. First she showed her how swollen her belly was, and how she couldn't close her dresses and skirts. She told her how in the morning when she got up, she felt sick and queasy. How her chest hurt so that nobody could touch it. And so, at last, she said, reluctantly, that perhaps, who knows, probably, most likely, it was because she was a little bit pregnant. Gertrudis heard this all calmly, not fazed by any of it. In the revolution she had seen and heard worse things than this.

"And tell me, does Rosaura know yet?"

"No, I don't know what she would do if she learned the truth."

"The truth! The truth! Look, Tita, the simple truth is that the truth does not exist; it all depends on a person's point of view. For example, in your case, the truth could be that Rosaura married Pedro, showing no loyalty, not caring a damn that you really loved him, that's the truth, isn't it?"

"Yes, but in fact she is his wife, not me."

"What does that matter! Did the wedding change the way you and Pedro truly feel?"

"No."

"To tell the truth, no! Of course not! Because this love is one of the truest loves I've ever seen. Pedro and you have both made the mistake of trying to keep the truth a secret, but it will come out in time. Look, Mama is dead, and it's God's own truth that she wouldn't listen to reason, but Rosaura is different, she knows the truth perfectly well and has to understand; what's more, I think that deep down she has always understood. You have no choice but to stand up for the truth, right now."

"You think I should talk to her?"

"Look, while I tell you what I would do in your place, why don't you fix the syrup for my fritters? Let's get a move on; the truth is it's getting late already."

Tita accepted her advice and began to prepare the syrup, without missing a single one of her sister's words. Gertrudis was sitting facing the kitchen door that led to the back patio, Tita was on the other side of the table, with her back to the door, so it was impossible for her to see Pedro walking toward the kitchen, carrying a bag of beans to feed the troop. Then Gertrudis, with the practiced eye she'd gained on the battlefield, made a strategic estimate of the time it would take Pedro to step over the threshold of the door, so that at that precise moment, she could fire these words:

". . . I think you should tell Pedro you're expecting his child."

A perfect hit, bull's eye! Pedro, struck down, let the sack fall to the floor. He was dying of love for Tita. Startled, she turned to discover that Pedro was looking at her, almost in tears.

"Pedro, what a coincidence! My sister has something to tell you. Why don't you go out to the garden to talk, while I finish the syrup?

Tita didn't know whether to chide or thank Gertrudis for her interference. She would talk to her later; right now she had no choice but to talk to Pedro. In silence, she handed Gertrudis the dish she had been holding, in which she had started to prepare the syrup, pulled a creased sheet of paper with the recipe written on it from a box on the table, and left it with Gertrudis in case she needed it. She walked out of the kitchen, Pedro following behind her.

Gertrudis needed the recipe; without it she'd be lost! Carefully, she began to read it and try to follow it:

" 'Beat an egg white in half a pint of water for each two pounds of sugar or *piloncillo*, two egg whites in a pint of water for five pounds of sugar, or in the same proportion for greater or lesser quantities. Boil the syrup until it bubbles up three times, slowing the boil with a little cold water, which is thrown in each time it starts to rise up. Then take it off the heat, let it stand, and skim off the foam; next add another little bit of water as well as a chunk of orange peel, anise, or clove to taste and bring to a boil. Skim it again, and when it has reached the stage of cooking called the ball stage, strain it through a sieve or a piece of linen stretched over a frame.' "

Gertrudis read this recipe as if she were reading hieroglyphics. She didn't know how much sugar was meant by five pounds, or what a pint of water was, much less what this ball business was. She was the one who was all balled up! She went out to the patio to ask Chencha for help.

Chencha had just finished serving beans to the congregation at the fifth breakfast mess. This was the last mess she had to serve, but as soon as she was done feeding them, she had to get ready for the next ones, since the revolutionaries who had received their sacred sustenance at the first breakfast mess were coming back to eat, and so on and so on, until ten at night, when she was done serving the last supper. For that reason it was perfectly understandable that she would be awfully angry and irritable at anyone who approached her to ask her to do any extra work. *Generala* though she was, Gertrudis was no exception. Chencha flatly refused to give her any assistance. She wasn't part of Gertrudis's troop, she didn't have to obey blindly like the men under her command.

Then Gertrudis was tempted to appeal to her sister, but her common sense stopped her. She could not disturb Tita and Pedro in any way at this time, perhaps the most critical moment of their lives.

Tita was slowly walking between the fruit trees in the garden, its smell of orange blossoms mingling with the jasmine scent always given off by her body. Pedro, at her side, was holding her arm tenderly.

"Why didn't you tell me?"

"I wanted to decide what to do first."

"And have you decided?"

"No."

"I think it would be good for you to know before you make a decision that for me, having a child with you is the best stroke of luck, and to enjoy it the way we should, I would like to go far away from here with you."

"We can't think only of ourselves, there are also Rosaura and Esperanza to consider. What's going to happen to them?"

Pedro couldn't answer. He hadn't thought of them until now, and to be honest he didn't want to hurt them, nor stop seeing his little girl. He had to have a solution fair to all of them. He would have to find one. At least there was one thing certain, Tita would not leave the ranch with John Brown.

A noise behind them made them jump. Someone was coming up behind them. Pedro dropped Tita's arm and turned his head furtively to see who it was. It was Pulque, who had gotten tired of listening to Gertrudis shouting in the kitchen and was looking for a better place to get some sleep. Anyway, they decided to postpone their conversation until another time. There were too many people all around the house; it was risky to talk about such private matters.

In the kitchen, Gertrudis wasn't having much success getting Sergeant Treviño to fix the syrup the way she wanted, no matter how many orders she gave him. She was sorry she had ever entrusted Treviño with such an important mission; when she had asked a group of rebels who knew how much a pound was and he had fired back the answer that a pound was 460 grams and a pint was a quarter of a liter, she thought he knew a lot about cooking, but he didn't.

In fact, this was the first time Treviño had ever failed in something with which she had entrusted him. She remembered one occasion when he had had to uncover a spy who had infiltrated the troop.

A prostitute who was the spy's mistress had learned of his activities, and before she could denounce him, he had gunned her down cold-bloodedly. Gertrudis was returning from taking a bath in the river and found her in the throes of death. The prostitute managed to gasp out a clue to identifying him. The traitor had a red mole shaped like a spider between his legs.

Gertrudis couldn't ask to inspect all the men in the troop, since not only could that be taken the wrong way, but the traitor could get suspicious and flee before they got to him. So she entrusted the mission to Treviño. Even for him it was no easy task. What they'd think about him was worse than what they'd think about her if he went prying into the crotches of all the men in the troop. So the patient Treviño waited until they got to Saltillo.

The minute they got to town he took on the job of going to every single brothel and gaining the confidence of every single prostitute, using who knew what kind of arts. But the main thing was that Treviño always treated them like ladies, he made them feel like queens. He was gallant and cultivated; he recited verses and poems while making love to them. Not a one had escaped his clutches, and they were all ready to work for the revolution.

In that way, with the help of his friends the whores,

it didn't take more than three days to uncover the traitor and set a trap for him. The traitor went into a room in the whorehouse with a peroxide blonde named "Husky-Voice." Treviño was waiting behind the door.

Treviño kicked the door shut and then, in an unprecedented display of violence, he killed the traitor, by beating him to death. When there was no more life left in him, Treviño cut off his testicles with a knife.

When Gertrudis asked him why he had murdered him so brutally and not simply dispatched him with a bullet, he replied that it had been an act of revenge. Years ago, a man who had a red mole in the shape of a spider between his legs had raped his mother and his sister. The latter had confessed before dying. So by doing this Treviño had restored the honor of his family. It was the only savage act Treviño committed in his life; except for that, he was refined and elegant, even in killing. He always did it with perfect dignity. After the capture of the spy, Treviño kept his reputation as a great womanizer. Which was not far from the truth; yet Gertrudis was ever the love of his life. He tried for months to conquer her—without success but never losing hope —until Gertrudis found Juan again. Then he realized that he had lost her forever. Now he was only her watchdog, protecting her flanks, not letting her out of sight for a second.

On the battlefield, he was one of her finest soldiers, but in the kitchen he wasn't good for very much. Still it would grieve Gertrudis to throw him out since Treviño was very emotional, and when she reprimanded him for anything he always took to drink. So she had no choice, she had to face up to her mistake in choosing him and try to make the best of it. Cautiously, the two of them read over the infernal recipe, step by step, trying to make sense of it.

" 'If the syrup is to be clarified, as it must be to sweeten liquors, after the previous procedures have been completed, tilt the pot or saucepan containing the syrup, let stand, and decant, or in other words, pour off as carefully as possible to separate the syrup from the sediment.' "

The recipe did not explain what the ball stage was, so Gertrudis ordered the sergeant to search for the answer in a huge cookbook that was in the storeroom.

Treviño was making a real effort to find the information they needed, but in fact he barely knew how to read; his finger slowly followed the words, as an impatient Gertrudis looked on.

" 'Candy syrup has many degrees of cooking: soft thread stage, firm thread stage, soft pearl stage, firm pearl stage, blowing stage, pouring stage, solidifying stage, and caramelizing stage, soft ball stage . . .' "

"Finally! Here's soft ball stage, General!"

"Let's see, bring it here! You've been driving me crazy."

Gertrudis read the instructions to her sergeant, quickly, in a loud voice:

" 'To test if the syrup is at the soft ball stage, moisten your fingers in a glass or jug of cold water and pick up some syrup, immediately dipping them back into the water. If the syrup forms a soft ball when it cools but handles like a paste, it is cooked to the soft ball stage.' Understand?"

"Yes, at least I think so, my general."

"You'd better, because if you don't I swear I'll have you shot!"

At last, Gertrudis had managed to gather all the information she'd been seeking; only one thing was left now and that was for the sergeant to do a good job making the syrup—then she could finally eat the fritters she craved so much.

Treviño was very much aware of the threat hanging over his head if he made a mistake while cooking for his superior; he completed his mission, despite his inexperience.

They were both ecstatic. Treviño was the happiest. He brought Tita a fritter himself, carried it up to her room on orders from Gertrudis to get Tita's stamp of approval. Tita hadn't come down for lunch and had spent the afternoon in bed. Treviño entered her bedroom and set the fritter down on a little table Tita used for just such occasions, when she ate there rather than in the dining room. She was grateful for his attentiveness and congratulated him, since the fritter really was delicious. Treviño said he was sorry Tita was indisposed; he would have been delighted to ask her to dance at the party being held on the patio to say good-bye to General Gertrudis. Tita assured him she would be delighted to dance with him, if she decided to come down to the party. Treviño withdrew quickly to go brag to the troops about what Tita had said.

As soon as the sergeant was gone, Tita lay down on her bed again. She had no desire to be anywhere else; her belly was too swollen, and she couldn't sit for very long.

Tita thought of the many times she had germinated

kernels or seeds of rice, beans, or alfalfa, without giving any thought to how it felt for them to grow and change form so radically. Now she admired the way they opened their skin and allowed the water to penetrate them fully, until they were split asunder to make way for new life. She imagined the pride they felt as the tip of the first root emerged from inside of them, the humility with which they accepted the loss of their previous form, the bravery with which they showed the world their new leaves. Tita would love to be a simple seed, not to have to explain to anyone what was growing inside her, to show her fertile belly to the world without laying herself open to society's disapproval. Seeds didn't have that kind of problem, they didn't have a mother to be afraid of or a fear of those who would judge them. Tita no longer had a mother but she couldn't get rid of the feeling that any minute some awful punishment was going to descend on her from the great beyond, courtesy of Mama Elena. That was a familiar feeling; it was like the fear she felt when she was cooking and didn't follow a recipe to the letter. She was always sure when she did it that Mama Elena would find out and, instead of congratulating her on her creativity, give her a terrible tongue-lashing for disobeying the rules. But she couldn't resist the temptation to violate the oh-so-rigid rules her mother imposed in the kitchen . . . and in life.

She stayed there resting for quite a while, lying on the bed; she only got up when she heard Pedro singing a love song beneath her window. Tita sprang to the window and threw it open. How could Pedro dare to be so brazen! As soon as she saw him, she knew the answer. She could tell at a glance he was roaring drunk. Juan, standing next to him, was accompanying him on the guitar.

Tita was in a panic; she hoped that Rosaura was already asleep—if she wasn't, there was going to be trouble!

A furious Mama Elena came into her room and said to her:

"See what you've done now? You and Pedro are shameless. If you don't want blood to flow in this house, go where you can't do any harm to anybody, before it's too late."

"The one who should be going is you. I'm tired of your tormenting me. Leave me in peace once and for all!"

"Not until you behave like a good woman, or a decent one at least!"

"What do you mean, decent? Like you?"

"Yes."

"But that's just what I'm doing! Or didn't you have an illicit child?"

"You will be condemned to hell for talking to me like this!"

"No more than you!"

"Shut your mouth! Who do you think you are?"

"I know who I am! A person who has a perfect right to live her life as she pleases. Once and for all, leave me alone; I won't put up with you! I hate you, I've always hated you!"

Tita had said the magic words that would make Mama Elena disappear forever. The imposing figure of her mother began to shrink until it became no more than a tiny light. As the ghost faded away, a sense of relief grew inside Tita's body. The inflammation in her belly and the pain in her breasts began to subside. The muscles at the center of her body relaxed, loosing a violent menstrual flow.

This discharge, so many days late, relieved all her pains. She gave a deep peaceful sigh. She wasn't pregnant.

But her problems weren't over. The little light, all that was left of Mama Elena's image, began to spin feverishly.

It went through the window and shot out onto the patio, like a firecracker out of control. Pedro, drunk as he was, didn't realize the danger. Cheerfully crooning "Estrellita" by Manuel M. Ponce, he stood under Tita's window surrounded by some rebels who were as drunk as he was. Gertrudis and Juan didn't see the danger approaching either. They were dancing like a pair of lovestruck teenagers by the glow of one of the many oil lamps set up on the patio to light up the party. The firecracker moved fast, approaching Pedro, whirling crazily, with enough violence to make the lamp closest to him explode into a thousand pieces. The oil quickly spread the flames onto Pedro's face and body.

Tita, who was taking measures to cope with her menstruation, heard the pandemonium set off by Pedro's accident. She rushed to the window, opened it, and saw Pedro running across the patio, like a human torch. Then, Gertrudis caught up with him, tearing the skirt from her dress, wrapping it around him, and knocking him to the ground.

Tita didn't know how she got down the stairs, but in less than twenty seconds she was at Pedro's side. As she arrived, Gertrudis was removing his smoldering clothes.

Pedro was howling in pain. He had burns over his whole body. Several men carefully lifted him between them to carry him to his bedroom. Tita, holding Pedro's unburnt hand, refused to leave his side. As they went up the stairs, Rosaura opened her bedroom door.

She noticed the smell of burnt feathers immediately. She went to the stairs, intending to go down and see what was happening, and there she found the group carrying Pedro, with him at the center in a cloud of smoke. Tita, at his side, was weeping uncontrollably. Rosaura's first impulse was to run and help her husband. Tita tried to let go of Pedro's hand so that Rosaura could get closer to him, but Pedro, between moans, cried out to her, addressing her familiarly for the first time:

"Tita, don't go. Don't leave me."

"No, Pedro, I won't."

Tita took Pedro's hand again. For a moment Rosaura and Tita looked at each other challengingly. Then Rosaura understood that there was nothing for her to do here, and she went back to her room and locked the door behind her. She didn't come back out for a week.

Since Tita didn't want to leave Pedro's side, she commanded Chencha to bring her lots of egg whites beaten with oil and finely grated raw potatoes. Those were the best ways she knew to deal with burns. The egg whites are applied very gently to the injured area, and reapplied each time the preparation dries. After this, plasters made of grated raw potatoes should be applied to reduce the inflammation and relieve the pain.

Tita spent the whole night dispensing these home remedies.

While she applied the potato plaster, she studied

Pedro's beloved face. There was no sign of his bushy eyebrows and his long eyelashes. His square chin was now an oval from the swelling. It didn't matter to Tita if he was left with scars, but it might to Pedro. How could she prevent scarring? Nacha gave her the answer, just as Morning Light had previously given it to her: in a case like this the best remedy was the bark of the tepezcohuite tree, which must be placed on Pedro. Tita went running out onto the patio; even though it was very late at night, she got Nicholas up and told him to get this bark, from the best *brujo* in the region. It was almost daybreak before she managed to soothe Pedro's pain a little, so that he was able to fall asleep for a moment. She took advantage of this opportunity to go out to say good-bye to Gertrudis, since she had been hearing movements and voices outside for quite a while, as the men in her troop saddled up their horses to get ready to go.

Gertrudis spoke with Tita for a long time, saying she was sorry she could not stay and help Tita in this misfortune, but her orders were to attack Zacatecas. Gertrudis thanked her sister for the happy moments she had spent with her, advised her not to give up the battle for Pedro, and before departing gave her a recipe the prostitutes use so they don't get pregnant: after having intimate relations, use a douche of boiled water with a few drops of vinegar. Juan came up and interrupted this conversation to tell Gertrudis it was time to leave.

Juan gave Tita a powerful embrace and told her to convey to Pedro his best wishes for his recovery. Tita and Gertrudis embraced each other, full of emotion. Gertrudis got onto her horse and rode away. She wasn't riding alone—she carried her childhood beside her, in the cream fritters she had enclosed in a jar in her saddle-bag.

Tita watched them go with tears in her eyes. Chencha did too, but unlike Tita's, hers were tears of joy. At last she'd get a rest!

When Tita was going back into the house, she heard Chencha scream:

"No! It can't be! They're coming back already."

In fact, it did look like someone from the troops was returning to the ranch, but it was hard to see who because of the dust the horses had raised as they left.

Straining her eyes, Tita was thrilled to see John's cart. He was back already. When she saw it, Tita felt completely confused. She didn't know what she was going to do or what she was going to tell him. Part of her felt an enormous joy at seeing him, but another part felt terrible at having to call off their engagement. John approached her with a huge bouquet of flowers. He embraced her warmly, but when he kissed her, he knew that something had changed inside of Tita.

TO BE CONTINUED . . .

Next month's recipe:

Beans with Chile Tezcucana-style

CHAPTER ELEVEN

November

Beans with Chile
Tezcucana-style

INGREDIENTS:

beans
pork
pork rinds
chiles anchos
onion
grated cheese
lettuce
avocado
radishes
chiles tornachiles
olives

PREPARATION:

First the beans have to be boiled with baking soda, and then washed and boiled again with pieces of pork and pork rind.

Putting the beans on to cook was the first thing Tita did when she got up at five in the morning.

Today she was expecting guests for dinner, John and his Aunt Mary, who had come from Pennsylvania just to attend John and Tita's wedding. Aunt Mary was anxious to meet her favorite nephew's fiancée and had not been able to because the timing was so unfortunate, with the state of Pedro's health. They had waited a week for him to recover before making a formal visit. Worried as Tita was, she could not cancel the meeting she owed to John's aunt, who was eighty years old and had traveled so far just to meet her. To give a good dinner to Aunt Mary was the least Tita could do for John and the old dear, but she had nothing to offer them except the announcement that she wasn't going to marry John. She felt completely empty, like a platter that held only crumbs, all that was left of a marvelous pastry. She looked for food in the pantry, but it was conspicuous by its absence; there really wasn't a thing. Gertrudis's visit to the ranch had laid waste to the larder. The only thing left in the granary, other than corn to make some tasty tortillas, was some rice and beans. But with a little imagination and a full heart one can always prepare a decent meal. A menu of rice, plantains, and beans Tezcucana-style isn't half bad.

As the beans weren't as fresh as they might be, she knew they would take more time than usual to cook, so she put them on early. As they cooked, she took care of the chiles anchos, removing their seeds and membranes.

After the chiles were deveined, she soaked them in warm water and finally pureed them.

As soon as the chiles were soaking, Tita fixed breakfast for Pedro and took it up to his room.

He was fairly recovered from his burns. Tita had not faltered in her application of tepezcohuite bark for so much as a moment, ensuring that Pedro would not be scarred. John had approved her treatment one hundred percent. Curiously, his grandmother, Morning Light, had begun experiments with this bark, and he himself had been continuing them for some time. Pedro was anxiously waiting for Tita. In addition to the delicious meals she brought him every day, another factor helped bring about his amazing recovery: the conversations he had with her after eating his meals. This morning Tita didn't have the time to devote to it, she wanted to make the meal for John the best she could. Pedro, his jealousy erupting, said to her:

"What you should do instead of inviting him to dinner is to tell him once and for all that you're not going to marry him because you are going to have my baby."

"I can't say that, Pedro."

"Why? Are you afraid you'll hurt your little doctor?"

"It's not that I'm afraid, but it would be so unjust to treat John that way, with all the respect I owe him; I have to wait for the best time to tell him."

"If you won't do it, I'll do it myself."

"No, you're not going to say anything to him; in the first place, because I won't allow it, and in the second, because I'm not pregnant."

"What? What do you mean?"

"What I thought was a pregnancy was just an irregularity; now I'm back to normal."

"So, is that it? Now I see what's going on. You don't want to talk to John because you're starting to have doubts about whether to stay with me or marry him, right? You aren't tied to me anymore, a poor sick man."

Tita couldn't understand Pedro's attitude; he was behaving like a child throwing a tantrum. He talked as if he was going to be sick for the rest of his days, but it wouldn't be that long—in a little while he'd be completely healed. Perhaps the accident he had suffered had affected his mind. Perhaps his head was full of the smoke his body had given off when it burned and just as burnt toast changes the way the whole house smells, making it unpleasant, so his smoky brain was producing these black thoughts, turning his usually pleasant words into awful ones. How could he doubt her, how could he mean to behave this way, contrary to the principle that had always governed his treatment of others—his sense of decency.

She left his room upset; Pedro, before the door was shut, yelled after her that she needn't come back to bring him his dinner, she should send Chencha, so she'd have as much time as she liked for seeing John.

Angry, Tita went into the kitchen and got her breakfast; she hadn't made it earlier because her first concern was to take care of Pedro and then her daily work—and all for what? So that Pedro could offend her with everything he said and did, not once considering her feelings. It was definitely true, Pedro had turned into a monster of selfishness and suspicion.

She prepared some chilaquiles and sat down at the kitchen table to eat them. She didn't like to eat alone, but when it came right down to it she had no choice, since Pedro couldn't get out of his bed; Rosaura didn't want to get out of hers and stayed shut up in her bedroom, hermetically sealed, not taking any meals; and Chencha, having had her first baby, had taken a few days off.

That's why the chilaquiles didn't taste as good as usual: for want of someone's company. Immediately she heard some footsteps. The door of the kitchen opened, and there stood Rosaura.

Tita was astonished at the sight of her. She was as thin as she had been when she was single. After just a week without eating! It seemed impossible that she had lost sixty-five pounds in just seven days, but so she had.

The same thing had happened when she had gone to live in San Antonio: she had become thin very quickly, but all she had to do was come back to the ranch and she got fat again!

Rosaura swept in and sat down facing Tita. It was time to confront her sister, but it wouldn't be Tita who would start the argument. She removed her plate, took a sip of her coffee, and began carefully breaking up the ends of the tortillas that she had used to make the chilaquiles.

They always cut off the edges of the tortillas they ate to throw them to the chickens. They crumbled the crusts from the hard rolls, too, for the same purpose. Rosaura and Tita stared unblinkingly at each other, and their eyes were still locked when Rosaura opened the discussion.

"I think you and I are overdue for a talk, don't you agree?"

"Yes, I certainly do. We have been ever since you married my boyfriend."

"Fine, if that's what you want, let's start there. With your wrongful claim to a boyfriend. You had no right to have a boyfriend."

"Says who? Is that according to Mama or to you?"

"According to family tradition, which you were breaking."

"And I'm going to break with it several more times if I have to, as long as this cursed tradition doesn't take me into account. I had the same right to marry as you did, and you had no right to stand between two people who were deeply in love."

"Not that deeply. You saw how Pedro switched to me

at the least opportunity. I married him because that's what he wanted. If you had had the tiniest scrap of pride, you would have put him out of your mind forever."

"Well for your information, he married you just so he could be near me. He doesn't love you, and you know that perfectly well."

"Look, it would be better if we didn't dig up the past; I don't care what Pedro's motives were in marrying me. The fact is he did. I'm not going to let you two make a fool of me, do you hear? I'm not about to let you do that."

"No one is trying to make a fool of you, Rosaura, you've got it all wrong."

"That is nonsense! I'm painfully aware of the role you put me in, when everybody on the ranch saw you weeping at Pedro's side, holding his hand so lovingly. Do you know what that role is? Laughingstock! You know, you really don't deserve God's mercy! As far as I'm concerned, I couldn't care less if you and Pedro go to hell for sneaking around kissing in every corner. From now on, you can do it all you want. As long as nobody finds out about it, I don't care, because Pedro is going to have to do it with someone who will, since as for me, he isn't going to put so much as a hand near me ever again. I, I have some self-respect left! Let him go to a loose woman like you for his filthy needs, but here's the thing: in this house I intend to go on being his wife. And in the eyes of everyone else, too. Because the day someone sees you two, and I end up looking ridiculous again, I swear that you are going to be very sorry."

Rosaura's shrieking was added to by Esperanza's insistent wailing. The baby had been crying for quite some time, but the volume of her sobs had been gradually increasing until it became unbearable. She must want something to eat. Rosaura rose slowly, saying:

"I am going to feed my daughter. From now on, I don't want you feeding her, never again, you'll stain her with your filth. All she can get from you is a bad example and bad advice."

"There's one thing for sure. I'm not going to allow you to poison your daughter with those sick ideas you have in your head. I'm not going to let you ruin her life either, forcing her to follow some stupid tradition!"

"Is that so? How are you going to stop me? You must think I'll let you stay as close to her as you are now, but mark my words, I won't. When have you ever seen streetwalkers allowed to mix with girls from decent families?"

"Don't tell me you seriously believe that this is a decent family!"

"My little family certainly is! That's why I will continue to keep you from getting anywhere near my daughter, or I will find it necessary to run you out of this house, which Mama left to me. Do you understand?"

Rosaura left the kitchen to feed Esperanza, taking the mush Tita had prepared for her. She couldn't have done anything worse to Tita. She had known how to hurt Tita most deeply.

Esperanza was one of the things Tita loved most in the world. The anguish she felt! As she tore apart the last little piece of tortilla left in her hand, she wished with all her heart that her sister would be swallowed up by the earth. That was the least she deserved.

All the while she was arguing with Rosaura she kept

breaking off chunks of tortilla, until she had divided them all into minuscule pieces. Tita angrily slid them onto a plate and went out to throw them to the chickens, so that she could get on with the preparation of the beans. All the clotheslines on the patio were full of Esperanza's snow-white diapers. They were the most beautiful diapers. They had all spent whole afternoons embroidering the borders. They swayed in the wind like foam-covered waves. Tita had to tear her eyes away from them. She had to forget that for the first time the child was eating without her if she wanted to be able to finish fixing dinner. She went back to the kitchen and set about preparing the beans.

The chopped onion is fried in lard. When it has turned golden brown, add the pureed chiles anchos to the pan and salt to taste.

After the broth is seasoned, add the beans with the pork and pork rinds.

It was hopeless to try to forget Esperanza. Pouring the beans into the pan, Tita remembered how much the child liked bean broth. To feed it to her, she sat her on her knees, spread a huge napkin over her front, and gave her the broth with a little silver spoon. How happy she had been the day she heard the sound of the spoon hitting against Esperanza's first tooth. Now two more were coming in. Tita was very careful not to hurt them when she was feeding her. She hoped that Rosaura would be, too. But how would she know, if she'd never done it before? She wouldn't know how to prepare her bath either, putting lettuce leaves in the water to make sure she slept peacefully at night; she wouldn't know how to dress her and kiss her and hug her and coo to her like Tita did. Tita thought it might be best for her to leave the ranch. She was disappointed in Pedro—and if Tita weren't in the house, Rosaura could start a new life; the baby had to get used to being cared for by her real mother sooner or later. If Tita kept getting more attached to her every day, she would end up suffering as she had with Roberto. She had no claim, it wasn't her family, and they could send her away at any moment, just as easily as one tosses away a stone while cleaning a pot of beans. John, in contrast, was offering her something different, the opportunity to establish a new family that no one could take away from her. He was a marvelous man; she loved him very much. As time went by, it wouldn't be hard to fall deeply in love with him.

She couldn't continue her reflections because the chickens were starting to make a huge ruckus on the patio. It seemed they'd gone mad or developed a taste for cock-fighting. They were giving little pecks at each other, trying to snatch away the last chunks of tortilla left on the ground. They hopped and flew wildly in every direction, launching violent attacks. Among the whole group, there was one that was in the greatest frenzy, using her beak to peck out the eyes of every hen she could, so that Esperanza's white diapers were sprayed with blood. Tita, stunned, tried to break up the fight, throwing a bucket of water over them. That only enraged them the more, raising the battle to a higher pitch. They formed a circle, each one setting dizzily upon the next. Soon the chickens were inescapably trapped by the force they themselves were generating in their mad chase; they couldn't break loose from that whirl of feathers, blood, and dust that spun faster and faster, gathering force at every turn until it changed into a mighty tornado, destroying everything in its path, starting with the things that were closest—in this case, Esperanza's diapers, hanging on the patio clotheslines. Tita tried to save a few diapers, but when she went to get them, she found herself being swept away by the force of the incredible whirlwind, which lifted her several feet off the ground and took her on three hellish orbits within the fury of beaks before flinging her onto the opposite end of the patio, where she landed like a sack of potatoes.

Tita stayed flat on the ground, terrified. She couldn't move. If she was caught in the whirlwind again, the chickens could peck her eyes out. That hen hurricane was boring a hole in the dirt of the patio, a hole so deep that most of the chickens disappeared from the face of the earth. The earth swallowed them up. After that fight only three chickens remained, plucked bald and one-eyed. And no diapers.

Tita, shaking the dust off of her, looked around the patio: there was no sign of the chickens. She was more worried about the disappearance of the diapers she had embroidered so lovingly. They had to be replaced with new ones right away. But then that was no longer her problem—hadn't Rosaura told her she didn't want her around Esperanza anymore? Let Rosaura tend to her concerns and Tita would tend to hers, which at the moment was getting dinner ready for John and his Aunt Mary.

She entered the kitchen and went to finish the preparation of the beans, but much to her surprise she found that the beans still weren't done, despite the hours they had been cooking.

Something strange was going on. Tita remembered

that Nacha had always said that when people argue while preparing tamales, the tamales won't get cooked. They can be heated day after day and still stay raw, because the tamales are angry. In a case like that, you have to sing to them, which makes them happy; then they'll cook. Tita supposed the same thing had happened with the beans, which had witnessed her fight with Rosaura. That meant all she could do was to try to improve their mood, to sing them a song full of love: she didn't have much time to finish preparing the meal for her guests.

The best thing was to try to remember a moment when she had felt great joy and relive it as she sang. She closed her eyes and began to sing a waltz that went: "I'm so happy since I have found you, I've surrendered my love to you, and given up my soul. . . ." Images from her first meeting with Pedro in the dark room flooded her mind. The passion with which Pedro had torn away her clothes, causing the flesh beneath her skin to burn beneath the touch of those incandescent hands. The blood simmered in her veins. Her heart burst into a seething passion. Very slowly the frenzy had subsided and given way to infinite tenderness, leaving their shaken souls satisfied.

While Tita was singing, the bean liquor was boiling madly. The beans allowed the liquid in which they were floating to penetrate them; they swelled until they were about to burst. When Tita opened her eyes and took a bean to test it, she saw that now the beans were done perfectly. That left enough time to get herself ready for Aunt Mary. Happy with life, she left the kitchen and went to her bedroom, intending to get dressed. The first thing she had to do was brush her teeth. The roll on the ground, when she'd been knocked over by the whirlwind of chickens, had left them full of dirt. She took some tooth powder and brushed them vigorously.

They had learned to prepare these powders in school. They're made by combining half an ounce cream of tartar, half an ounce of sugar, and half an ounce of jivia bone with two drachmas of Florentine iris and dragon's blood, reducing all the ingredients to a powder, and blending well. Jovita, their teacher, was in charge of making it. She was their teacher for three years in a row. She was a small, slight woman. They all remembered her not so much for what she had taught them, but because she was such a character. They say she'd been left a widow at eighteen, with a baby. No one wanted to become stepfather to this child, which is why she had chosen to spend her life entirely celibate. Who knows how she adopted that resolution or how it affected her; as the years went by, the poor thing went completely out of her mind. She struggled night and day to put a stop to bad thoughts. Her favorite saying was "Idle hands are the devil's playground." She never rested a moment the entire day. She worked more and slept less all the time. In time, the work inside her house wasn't enough to put her spirit at rest, so she was out on the street at five every morning to sweep the sidewalk. Her own and her neighbors. Then she expanded her field of action to the four blocks around her house and so on, gradually, until, *in crescendo*, she was sweeping all of Piedras Negras before going to school. Sometimes she still had bits of garbage clinging to her skin, and the students laughed at her. In the mirror, Tita saw that she looked like her teacher.

Perhaps it was just the feathers matted in her hair because of her fall; but still, she was horrified.

She didn't want to become another Jovita. She removed the feathers, gave her hair a vigorous brushing, and went down to receive John and Mary, who were just arriving. Pulque's barking had announced their presence.

Tita received them in the living room. Aunt Mary was just as she had imagined her: a polite, pleasant elderly lady. Despite her years, she was impeccably turned out.

She was wearing an understated floral hat, in a pastel color, that contrasted with the white of her hair. Her gloves matched her hair, gleaming snow-white. She carried a mahogany walking stick with a silver head shaped like a swan. Her conversation was absolutely charming. The aunt pronounced herself delighted with Tita; she went on at length about her nephew's excellent choice and Tita's perfect English.

Tita made her sister's excuses for not being present, saying she was indisposed, and invited them to move into the dining room.

The aunt was delighted with the rice with fried plantains and praised the bean dish to the heavens.

When the beans are served, they are covered with grated cheese and garnished with tender lettuce leaves, avocado slices, chopped radishes, chiles tornachiles, and olives.

The aunt was used to a different type of food, but that did not prevent her from being able to appreciate the wonderful meal Tita had prepared.

"Mmmm. It's delicious, Tita."

"Thank you."

"You are lucky, Johnny, to be eating well from now on, because to tell the truth Katy is a very bad cook. Marriage is going to fatten you up."

John could see that Tita was upset.

"Is something the matter, Tita?"

"Yes, but I can't tell you right now, your aunt would feel bad if we stopped speaking English."

John answered her, speaking in Spanish.

"No, don't worry, she's completely deaf."

"Then how can she talk with us?"

"She reads lips, but don't worry, she only reads English. Besides, when she's eating, she doesn't know us from Adam, so for pity's sake tell me what's the matter. We haven't had a chance to talk and we're getting married in less than a week."

"John, I think we'd better call it off."

"But why?"

"Don't make me tell you now."

Tita smiled, trying not to let the aunt see they were discussing a rather delicate topic. The aunt smiled too, obviously perfectly happy, quite satisfied eating her plate of beans. It was clear, she really couldn't read their lips in Spanish. Tita could talk to John without any danger. John stuck to the subject.

"Don't you love me anymore?"

"I don't know."

It was hard for Tita to go on speaking when she saw the look of sorrow that came over John, which he immediately tried to control.

"While you were gone, I had relations with a man I've always loved, and I lost my virginity. That's the reason, I can't marry you anymore."

After a long silence, John asked:

"Are you more in love with him or with me?"

"I can't answer that, I just don't know. When you aren't here, I think he is the one I love, but when I see you, everything changes. Near you I feel calm, settled, at peace. . . . But I don't know, I don't know. . . . Forgive me for telling you all this."

Two tears were sliding down Tita's cheeks. Aunt Mary took her hand, very moved, and said in English:

"How wonderful to see a woman in love weeping with emotion. I did the same many times when I was about to get married."

John realized that these words could make Tita burst into tears and that then the situation would be out of control.

He reached out and took Tita's hand and said, with a smile on his face to agree with his aunt's:

"Tita, it doesn't matter to me what you did, there are some things in life that shouldn't be given so much importance, if they don't change what is essential. What you've told me hasn't changed the way I think; I'll say again, I would be delighted to be your companion for the rest of your life—but you must think over very carefully whether I am the man for you or not. If your answer is yes, we will celebrate our wedding in a few days. If it's no, I will be the first to congratulate Pedro and ask him to give you the respect you deserve."

John's words didn't surprise Tita; they reflected his character. What surprised her was that he knew without a doubt that his rival was Pedro. She had not reckoned on his uncanny intuition.

Tita could not remain at the table. Excusing herself,

she ran to the patio for a moment, where she cried until she calmed back down. She returned in time to serve dessert. John rose to push in her chair and treated her with the same tenderness and respect as always. What a fine man he was. How he had grown in her eyes! And how the doubts had grown inside her head! The jasmine sorbet she served for dessert provided a great relief. Swallowing it, her body was refreshed, her mind cleared. The aunt was crazy about the dessert. She had never imagined that jasmine flowers could be eaten. Intrigued, she wanted to know exactly how to prepare a sorbet just like it at home. Very slowly, so the aunt could read her lips clearly, Tita gave her the recipe.

"Crush a sprig of jasmine and put it in three pints of water with a half pound of sugar, mixing well. When the sugar is completely dissolved, strain the mixture through a piece of linen stretched over a container and then place it in the ice-cream maker to freeze."

The rest of the afternoon went wonderfully. As John was leaving, he gave Tita a kiss on the hand, saying:

"I don't want to put any pressure on you, I just want to assure you that you would be happy with me."

"I know."

Of course she knew. Of course she was going to take that into account when she made her decision, that crucial decision that would determine her whole future.

TO BE CONTINUED . . .

Next month's recipe:

Chiles in Walnut Sauce

CHAPTER TWELVE

DECEMBER

Chiles in Walnut Sauce

INGREDIENTS:

25 chiles poblanas
8 pomegranates
100 cashew nuts
100 grams aged fresh cheese
1 kilo ground steak
100 grams raisins
1/4 kilo almonds
1/4 kilo walnuts
1/2 kilo tomatoes
2 medium onions
2 candied citrons
1 peach
1 apple
cumin
white pepper
salt
sugar

PREPARATION:

Begin shelling the nuts several days in advance, for that is a big job, to which many hours must be devoted. After the nut is taken from the shell, you still have to remove the skin that covers the nut. Take care that none of this skin, not a single bit, is left clinging to the nuts, because when they're ground and mixed with the cream, any skin will make the nut sauce bitter, and all of your previous work will have been for nothing.

Tita and Chencha were finishing shelling the nuts, sitting around the kitchen table. The nuts were to be used for the chiles in nut sauce they would be serving as the main course at the next day's wedding. All the other members of the family had gone, deserting the kitchen table on one pretext or another. Only those two indefatigable women were continuing to the bottom of the mountain. To tell the truth, Tita didn't blame the others. They had given her enough help already this week; she knew quite well that it wasn't easy to shell a thousand nuts without getting sick of it. The only person she knew who could do it without any sign of fatigue was Mama Elena.

Not only could she crack sack after sack of nuts in a short time, she seemed to take great pleasure in doing it.

Applying pressure, smashing to bits, skinning, those were among her favorite activities. The hours just flew by when she sat on the patio with a sack of nuts between her legs, not getting up until she was done with it.

For her it would have been child's play to crack those thousand nuts, which required so much effort from everyone else. They needed that enormous quantity because for each 25 chiles they had to shell 100 nuts; so it figured that for 250 chiles, they needed 1,000 nuts. They had invited eighty people to the wedding, between relatives and close friends. Each one could eat three chiles if they wanted, a fairly generous estimate. This was to be a quiet wedding; nonetheless, Tita wanted to give a twenty-course banquet the likes of which had never been given before, and of course she couldn't leave the delicious chiles in walnut sauce off of the menu, even though they took so much work—such a memorable occasion surely warranted it. It didn't matter to Tita if she had black fingers after taking the skin off so many nuts. This wedding was well worth the sacrifice—it had a special significance for her. For John too. He was so happy that he had been one of her most enthusiastic helpers in the preparation of the banquet. Indeed, he had been one of the last to stop to rest. He deserved a good rest.

At home in his bathroom, John was washing his

hands, dead tired. His fingernails hurt from peeling so many nuts. Getting ready for bed, he was filled with intense emotion. In a few hours he would be closer to Tita, and that gave him enormous satisfaction. The wedding was scheduled for midday. He looked at his smoking jacket, draped over a chair. Everything he would wear was meticulously arranged, waiting for the moment to dress. The shoes shone their brightest; the bow tie, sash, and shirt were impeccable. Satisfied that everything was in order, he took a deep breath, lay down and, as soon as his head touched the pillow, was sound asleep.

Pedro, on the other hand, could not get to sleep. A terrible jealousy gnawed at his entrails. He didn't care at all for the idea of going to the wedding and having to endure seeing Tita together with John.

He couldn't understand John's attitude at all; he acted like he had mush in his veins. John knew perfectly well what was between Tita and him. Yet he acted as if it were nothing. That afternoon, when Tita was trying to light the oven, she couldn't find any matches anywhere. John, always gallant, had quickly offered to help her. But that wasn't all! After lighting the fire, he had presented Tita with the box of matches, taking her hands in his. What business did he have giving Tita that kind of ridiculous gift? It was just a pretext for John to stroke Tita's hands in front of Pedro. John thought he was so civilized —he'd teach him what a man does when he really loves a woman. Grabbing his jacket, he got ready to go look for John so he could smash his face in.

He stopped at the door. He couldn't contribute to any vicious talk about how Tita's brother-in-law had gotten in a fight with John the day before the wedding.

Tita would never forgive him. Angrily, he threw his jacket on the bed and went looking for a pill for his headache. The noise Tita made in the kitchen was magnified a thousand times by the pain.

Tita was thinking of her sister as she finished shelling the last few nuts left on the table. Rosaura would have enjoyed this wedding so much. The poor thing had been dead for a year. They had waited all this time to hold the religious ceremony in honor of her memory. Her death had been extremely odd. She had eaten supper as usual and immediately afterward had gone to her room. Esperanza and Tita had sat talking for a while in the dining room. Pedro had gone upstairs to say good night to Rosaura before going to sleep. Tita and Esperanza couldn't hear a thing, the dining room was so far from the bedrooms. At first Pedro didn't find it odd that he could hear Rosaura breaking wind even with the door closed. He began to notice the unpleasant noises when one lasted so long it seemed it would never end. Pedro tried to concentrate on the book he was holding, thinking that drawn-out sound could not possibly be the product of his wife's digestive problems. The floor was shaking, the light blinked off and on. Pedro thought for a moment it was the rumble of cannons signaling that the revolution had started up again, but he discarded the thought; it had been too calm in the country lately. Maybe it was the engine of one of the neighbor's motorcars. But motorcars didn't produce such a nauseating smell. How strange that he could smell it even though he'd taken the precaution of walking all around the bedroom with a spoon containing a chunk of burning charcoal and a pinch of sugar.

That was the most effective remedy against bad smells.

When he was a child, it was what they always did in the room where someone had had the stomach flu, and it had always worked to fumigate the atmosphere. This time it hadn't done a bit of good. Worried, he went over to the door that communicated between the two bedrooms; tapping with his knuckles, he asked Rosaura if she felt all right. Receiving no answer, he opened the door: there he found Rosaura, her lips purple, body deflated, eyes wild, with a distant look, sighing out her last flatulent breath. John's diagnosis was an acute congestion of the stomach.

Her burial was very poorly attended, because the disagreeable odor Rosaura's body gave off got worse after her death. For that reason not many people chose to attend. The ones determined not to miss it were the buzzards—a flock of them circled the funeral party until the body had been buried. Seeing they weren't going to have a banquet, they flew off disappointed, leaving Rosaura to rest in peace.

But Tita's hour of rest had not yet come. Her body may have been crying for sleep, but she had to finish the walnut sauce first. That's why, instead of thinking about the past, it would be a lot better to hurry up with the cooking so she could take a well-deserved breather.

After the nuts have been peeled, grind them on the stone with the cheese and cream. Finally, add salt and white pepper to taste. Cover the filled chiles with this nut sauce and garnish with the pomegranates.

FILLING THE CHILES:

Fry the onions in a little oil. When they start to get transparent, add the ground meat, cumin, and a little sugar. After the meat has browned, stir in the chopped peach, apple, walnuts, raisins, almonds, and tomatoes until it's seasoned. When it's ready, add salt to taste and let the liquids cook off before removing from the heat.

Roast and peel the chiles separately. Slice them open on one side and take out the seeds and membranes.

Tita and Chencha finished garnishing the twenty-five trays of chiles and put them in a cool place. The next morning they would still be in perfect condition when the waiters would get them out and carry them in to the banquet.

The waiters were running from one side to the next serving the lively crowd of guests. When Gertrudis arrived at the party, she got everyone's attention. She drove up in a model T Ford coupe, one of the first to be produced with multiple gears. Stepping out of the car, she nearly dropped the huge wide-brimmed hat trimmed with ostrich feathers that she was carrying. Her dress with its shoulder pads was the most daring, absolutely the latest thing. Juan wasn't one to be left behind. He was sporting an elegant tight-fitting suit, a top hat, and spats. Their oldest child had turned into a fine figure of a mulatto. He had delicate features, and his clear blue eyes stood out against his dark skin. He got his dark skin from his grandfather and his blue eyes from Mama Elena. He had eyes just like his grandmother. Behind them came

Sergeant Treviño, who had been hired as a personal bodyguard by Gertrudis after the revolution.

At the entrance to the ranch Nicholas and Rosalio, in fancy charro costumes, were collecting invitations from the guests as they were arriving. The invitations were beautiful. Alex and Esperanza had prepared them personally. The paper used for the invitations, the black ink used to write them, the gold tint used on the edges of the envelopes, and the wax used to seal them—all those were their pride and joy. Everything had been prepared the traditional way, using the De la Garza family recipes. But they hadn't needed to prepare the black ink, for enough remained from the ink that had been made for Pedro and Rosaura's wedding. It was dried ink; all that had to be done was to add a little water and it was as good as new. The ink is made by mixing eight ounces of gum arabic, five and a half ounces of gall, four ounces of iron sulfate, two and a half ounces of logwood, and half an ounce of copper sulfate. To make the gold tint used on the edges of the envelopes, take an ounce of orpiment and an ounce of rock crystal, finely ground. Stir these powders into five or six well-beaten egg whites until the mixture is like water. And finally, the sealing wax is made by melting a pound of gum arabic, half a pound of benzoin, half a pound of calafonia, and a pound of vermilion.

When this mixture has liquefied, pour it onto a table greased with sweet almond oil and form into thin sticks or rods before it cools.

Esperanza and Alex spent many afternoons following these recipes to the letter so they could make invitations that were unique, and in that they had succeeded. Each was a work of art. They were the product of crafts that have, unfortunately, gone out of style, like long dresses, love letters, and the waltz. But for Tita and Pedro the waltz "The Eyes of Youth," which the orchestra was playing at Pedro's request, would never go out of style. Together they glided around the dance floor, bursting with style. Tita looked splendid. The twenty-two years that had passed since Pedro married Rosaura had not even touched her. At thirty-nine she was still as sharp and fresh as a cucumber that had just been cut.

As they danced, John followed them with his eyes, with a look full of affection and just a hint of resignation. Tenderly Pedro touched his cheek to Tita's, and his hand on her waist felt hotter than ever.

"Do you remember when we heard this song for the first time?"

"I'll never forget."

"I couldn't sleep that night, thinking about asking for your hand right then. I didn't know that it would take twenty-two years before I would ask you to be my wife."

"Are you asking me seriously?"

"Of course. I don't want to die without making you mine. I have always dreamed of walking with you into a church full of white flowers, and you the most beautiful of them all."

"Dressed in white?"

"Of course! There's nothing to stop you. And do you know what? Once we're married, I'd like to have a child wi h you. We still have time, don't you think? Now that Esperanza is leaving us, we'll need some company."

Tita couldn't answer Pedro. A lump in her throat prevented it. The tears slowly rolled down her cheeks. Her first tears of joy.

"And I want you to know that you can't convince me not to do it. I don't care what my daughter or anybody else thinks. We've spent too many years worrying about what people will say; from now on nothing is going to keep me away from you."

In fact, Tita no longer gave a damn either about what people would say when their love affair was made public.

For twenty years she had respected the pact the two of them had made with Rosaura; now she had had enough of it. Their pact consisted of taking into consideration the fact that it was vital to Rosaura to maintain the appearance that her marriage was going splendidly, and the most important thing for her was that her daughter grow up within that sacred institution, the family—the only way, she felt, to provide a firm moral foundation. Pedro and Tita had sworn to be absolutely discreet about their meetings and keep their love a secret. In the eyes of others, theirs must always be a perfectly normal family. For this to succeed, Tita must agree to give up having an illicit child. In compensation, Rosaura was prepared to share Esperanza with her, as follows: Tita would be in charge of feeding the child, Rosaura of her education.

Rosaura's side of the bargain was that she was required to live with them on friendly terms, avoiding jealousy and complaints.

For the most part, they had all observed the treaty, though it was least successful in respect to Esperanza's education. Tita wanted Esperanza to have a different education from the one Rosaura had planned for her. So even though it wasn't part of the deal, she took advantage of the moments Esperanza spent with her to provide the child with a different sort of knowledge than her mother was teaching her.

Those moments added up to most of the day, for the kitchen was Esperanza's favorite place and Tita was her best friend and confidante.

It was during one of these afternoons in the kitchen when Tita learned that Alex, John Brown's son, was courting Esperanza. Tita was the first to know. He had seen Esperanza again, after many years, at a party at the school she was attending. Alex was finishing medical school. They were attracted the moment they met. When Esperanza told Tita that when she felt Alex's eyes on her body, she felt like dough being plunged in boiling oil, Tita knew that Alex and Esperanza would be bound together forever.

Rosaura tried everything to prevent it. From the first, she was flatly and frankly opposed. Pedro and Tita pleaded Esperanza's case, which started a struggle to the death between them. Rosaura insisted loudly upon her rights: Pedro and Tita had broken the pact; it wasn't fair.

It wasn't the first time they had argued about Esperanza. That had been when Rosaura insisted that her daughter shouldn't attend school, since it would be a waste of time. If Esperanza's only lot in life was to take care of her mother forever, she didn't have any need for fancy ideas; what she needed was to study piano, singing, and dancing. Mastering those talents would be tremendously useful, first of all, because Esperanza could provide Rosaura with marvelous afternoons of entertainment and amusement, and second, because she would stand out at society balls for her spectacular performance. She would captivate everyone and would always be welcome among the upper class. With great effort, after three long conversations, they managed to convince Rosaura that besides singing, dancing, and performing at the piano, Esperanza need to be able to talk about interesting subjects when she was around, and for that she had to go to school. Very reluctantly, Rosaura agreed to send her daughter to school, but only because she had been convinced that Esperanza would not just learn how to make agreeable and amusing conversation there, but would mingle with the cream and upper crust of Piedras Negras society in grade school. Esperanza went to the best school, with the object of improving her mind. Tita, for her part, taught her something just as valuable: the secrets of love and life as revealed by the kitchen.

That victory over Rosaura had been enough to prevent another serious argument until now, when Alex was introduced and with him the possibility of an engagement. Rosaura was furious when she saw that Pedro and Tita were staunchly behind Esperanza. She fought with everything she had, she fought like a lioness to defend what according to tradition was her right—a daughter who would stay with her until she died. She kicked, she screamed, she yelled, she spit, she threw up, she made desperate threats. For the first time, she broke their pact and hurled curses at Pedro and Tita, holding up to them all the suffering they had caused her.

The house became a battlefield. Slammed doors were the order of the day. Fortunately this did not go on for long, because after three days of the most violent and heartrending battle between the two sides, Rosaura, due to her terrible digestive problems, had died of . . . whatever she had died of.

Having brought off the wedding between Alex and Esperanza was Tita's greatest triumph. How proud she felt to see Esperanza so self-confident, so intelligent, so perfectly prepared, so happy, so capable, and at the same time, so feminine and womanly, in the fullest sense of the word. She looked so beautiful in her wedding gown, waltzing with Alex to "The Eyes of Youth."

When the music was over, the Lobos, Paquita and Jorge, came up to congratulate Pedro and Tita.

"Congratulations, Pedro, your daughter couldn't have found a better match than Alex for ten miles around."

"Yes, Alex Brown is a wonderful boy. The only sad thing is that they're not going to stay with us. Alex won a grant to get his doctorate at Harvard University, and they're leaving for there today, right after the wedding."

"How awful, Tita! What are you going to do now?" inquired Paquita venomously. "Without Esperanza in the house you're not going to be able to live with Pedro. Oh, but before you move someplace else, give me the recipe for these chiles in walnut sauce. How exquisite they look!"

The chiles not only looked good, they were indeed delicious—never before had Tita done such a marvelous job with them. The platters of chiles proudly wore the colors of the flag: the green of the chiles, the white of the nut sauce, the red of the pomegranates.

These tricolored trays didn't last very long: the chiles disappeared in the blink of an eye . . . how long ago it seemed that Tita had felt like a chile in nut sauce left sitting on the platter out of etiquette, for not wanting to look greedy.

Tita wondered whether the fact that there was not a single chile left on the platters was a sign that good manners had been forgotten or that the chiles were indeed splendid.

Her fellow diners were delighted. What a difference between this wedding and that unfortunate day when Pedro and Rosaura got married, when all the guests had been overcome by food poisoning. Today, instead of feeling a terrible longing and frustration, they felt quite different; tasting these chiles in walnut sauce, they all experienced a sensation like the one Gertrudis had when she ate the quails in rose sauce. Again Gertrudis was the first to feel the symptoms. She was in the middle of the patio, dancing with Juan to "My Beloved Captain," and as she danced, she outdid herself singing the refrain. Every time she sang "Ay, ay, ay, ay, my beloved captain," she remembered that distant day when Juan was a captain and she met him in the open field, completely naked. She immediately recognized the heat in her limbs, the tickling sensation in the center of her body, the naughty thoughts, and she decided to leave with her husband before things went too far. When she left, .the party started to break up. All the other guests quickly made their excuses, coming up with one pretext or another, throwing heated looks at each other; they too left. The newlyweds were secretly delighted since this left them free to grab their suitcases and get away as soon as possible. They needed to get to the hotel.

Before Tita and Pedro knew it, along with John and Chencha, they were the only ones left on the ranch.

Everyone else, including the ranch hands, was making mad passionate love, wherever they had happened to end up. Some, under the bridge between Piedras Negras and Eagle Pass. The more conservative, in their cars, hastily pulled over to the side of the road. The rest, wherever they could. Any spot would do: in the river, on the stairs, under the washtub, in the fireplace, in the oven of the stove, under the counter in the drugstore, in the clothes closet, on a treetop. Necessity is the mother of invention, and of every position. That day it led to some of the greatest creativity in the history of the human race.

For their part, Tita and Pedro were making a powerful effort to keep their sexual impulses under control, but they were so strong that they went right through their skin and came out in the form of heat and a distinctive smell. John noticed and, seeing that he was the third wheel, said good-bye and left. It hurt Tita to see him go off alone. John should have found someone else when she refused him, but he never had.

After John left, Chencha asked permission to go to her village: it had been several days since her husband left to build a house there, and she had suddenly gotten a strong urge to visit him.

For the first time in their lives, Tita and Pedro could make love freely. For years they had had to take all sorts of precautions so that no one would see them, so that no one would suspect them, so that Tita would not become pregnant, so that she wouldn't cry out with pleasure when they were inside each other. But all that was over now.

With no need for words, they took each other's

hands and went into the dark room. Before entering, Pedro took her in his arms, slowly opened the door, and before his eyes the dark room was completely transformed. All the furniture had disappeared. There was just the brass bed standing royally in the middle of the room. The silk sheets and bedspread were white, like the floral rug that covered the floor and the 250 candles that lit up the now inappropriately named dark room. Tita was moved at the thought of the work that Pedro had done to prepare the room in this way, and so was Pedro, thinking how clever she had been to arrange it all in secret.

They were so filled with pleasure that they didn't notice that in a corner of the room Nacha lit the last candle, raised her finger to her lips as if asking for silence, and faded away.

Pedro placed Tita on the bed and slowly removed her clothing, piece by piece. After caressing each other, gazing at each other with infinite passion, they released the passion that had been contained for so many years.

The striking of the brass headboard against the wall and the guttural sounds that escaped from both of them mixed with the sound of the thousand doves flying free above them. Some sixth sense had told the doves that it was time to flee the ranch. With them fled all the other animals—the cows, the pigs, the chickens, the quails, the lambs, the horses.

Tita was aware of none of it. She was experiencing a climax so intense that her closed eyes glowed, and a brilliant tunnel appeared before her.

She remembered then the words that John had once spoken to her: "If a strong emotion suddenly lights all the candles we carry inside ourselves, it creates a brightness that shines far beyond our normal vision and then a splendid tunnel appears that shows us the way that we forgot when we were born and calls us to recover our lost divine origin. The soul longs to return to the place it came from, leaving the body lifeless." . . . Tita checked her passion.

She didn't want to die. She wanted to explore these emotions many more times. This was just the beginning.

She tried to still her breathing, and only then did she hear the flutter of the wings of the last doves as they flew off. Apart from that sound she heard only their hearts beating fiercely. She could feel Pedro's heart pounding against her chest. Suddenly the pounding ceased. A mortal silence spread through the room. It took her but a moment to realize that Pedro was dead.

With Pedro died the possibility of ever again lighting her inner fire, with him went all the candles. She knew that the natural heat that she was now feeling would cool little by little, consuming itself as rapidly as if it lacked fuel to maintain itself.

Surely Pedro had died at the moment of ecstasy when he entered the luminous tunnel. She regretted not having done the same. Now it would never again be possible to see that light, because she could no longer feel anything. She would but wander through the shadows for eternity, alone, all alone. She would have to find some way, even if it was an artificial one, of striking a fire that would light the way back to her origin and to Pedro. But first she had to thaw the freezing chill that was beginning to paralyze her. She got up and went running to the enormous bedspread that she had woven through night after night of solitude and insomnia, and she threw it over her. It covered the whole ranch, all three hectares. She pulled from her bureau drawer the box of candles that John had given her. She needed to have plenty of fuel in her body. She began to eat the candles out of the box one by one. As she chewed each candle she pressed her eyes shut and tried to reproduce the most moving memories of her and Pedro. The first time she saw him, the first time their hands touched, the first bouquet of roses, the first kiss, the first caress, the first time they made love. In this she was successful; when the candle she chewed made contact with the torrid images she evoked, the candle began to burn. Little by little her vision began to brighten until the tunnel again appeared before her eyes. There at its entrance was the luminous figure of Pedro waiting for her. Tita did not hesitate. She let herself go to the encounter, and they wrapped each other in a long embrace; again experiencing an amorous climax, they left together for the lost Eden. Never again would they be apart.

At that moment the fiery bodies of Pedro and Tita began to throw off glowing sparks. They set on fire the bedspread, which ignited the entire ranch. The animals had fled just in time to save themselves from the inferno! The dark room was transformed into an erupting volcano. It cast stone and ash in every direction. When the stones reached high enough, they exploded into multicolored lights. From miles away, people in neighboring towns watched the spectacle, thinking it was fireworks celebrating the wedding of Alex and Esperanza. But when the fires continued for a week, they came to get a closer look.

A layer of ash several yards high covered the entire ranch. When Esperanza, my mother, returned from her wedding trip, all that she found under the remains of what had been the ranch was this cookbook, which she bequeathed to me when she died, and which tells in each of its recipes this story of a love interred.

They say that under those ashes every kind of life flourished, making this land the most fertile in the region.

❖

Throughout my childhood I had the good fortune to savor the delicious fruits and vegetables that grew on that land. Eventually my mother had a little apartment building built there. My father Alex still lives in one of the apartments. Today he is going to come to my house to celebrate my birthday. That is why I am preparing Christmas Rolls, my favorite dish. My mama prepared them for me every year. My mama! . . . How wonderful the flavor, the aroma of her kitchen, her stories as she prepared the meal, her Christmas Rolls! I don't know why mine never turn out like hers, or why my tears flow so freely when I prepare them—perhaps I am as sensitive to onions as Tita, my great-aunt, who will go on living as long as there is someone who cooks her recipes.